Becca at Sea

Becca at Sea

~~~~~~

Deirdre Baker

GROUNDWOOD BOOKS
HOUSE OF ANANSI PRESS
TORONTO   BERKELEY

An excerpt from this book ("Seafire") was originally published (as "The
Cousins") in *Girls' Own: An Anthology of Canadian Fiction for Young Readers*,
edited by Sarah Ellis (Penguin, 2001).

Groundwood Books / House of Anansi Press
110 Spadina Avenue, Suite 801, Toronto, Ontario M5V 2K4

or c/o Publishers Group West
1700 Fourth Street, Berkeley, CA 94710

We acknowledge for their financial support of our publishing program
the Canada Council for the Arts, the Government of Canada through the
Book Publishing Industry Development Program (BPIDP)
and the Ontario Arts Council.

ONTARIO ARTS COUNCIL
CONSEIL DES ARTS DE L'ONTARIO

Library and Archives Canada Cataloguing in Publication
Baker, Deirdre F. (Deirdre Frances)
Becca at sea / Deirdre Baker.
ISBN-13: 978-0-88899-737-1 (bound) –
ISBN-10: 0-88899-737-X (bound) –
ISBN-13: 978-0-88899-738-8 (pbk.) –
ISBN-10: 0-88899-738-8 (pbk.)
I. Title.
PS8603.A455B43 2007   jC813'.6   C2007-902040-2

Cover illustration by Kim LaFave
Design by Michael Solomon
Printed and bound in Canada

For Bob Gibbs
Sine quo non

1. Seventeen Pearls

~~~~~~

"COME, Becca," said Gran.

"Just a minute," Rebecca said. She waved to her parents as the ferry chugged across the channel, taking them away to Tribune Island, then Vancouver Island, then Vancouver, and then to the trip in Europe.

"Becca, it's time to come," Gran said.

Not that Becca minded. It was just that she'd never stayed with Gran in February before, and with Mum and Dad so far away. And missing school! That was strange, too. And no aunts around to make life interesting, or uncles. No cousins. Well, that might be a good thing. No friends. But she was used to that on Gran's island, where all the kids were either teenagers or babies.

"I have to feed the cat," Gran said.

Becca wasn't afraid, but she was used to summer. She was used to having neighbors on the beach, and Dad and the aunts keeping Gran busy with arguments that were sometimes cheerful and sometimes not, and long light evenings when she and Mum went fishing, casting off the point even though trolling in a boat was really the way to catch salmon. She was used to long drawn-out sunsets when she sneaked up to the allotment gardens and Kay from next door fed her sweet carrots pulled straight from the earth.

But now it was already dim when they arrived at the cabin, and it was hardly dinnertime.

"Come on, Frank!" Gran called to the cat. "Becca's going to give you dinner!"

The cabin was cold, and Gran built a fire in the stove. They ate toast and eggs at the table by the window, but Becca couldn't even see the bay. Only her own reflection moved in the darkness, as if night were a wall that shut out the beach, the sea, and all the islands and mountains across the water.

"It's misting up," Gran said when she came back from the woodpile.

Becca fiddled with the little bottle that held the pearls Gran had collected over the years. Mum had pearls, too — a necklace that she wore when she and Dad went out somewhere fancy. Mum's pearls were perfectly round, and elegant and party-like. They made Becca think of beautiful clothes and perfume.

Gran's pearls were small as blackberry seeds, nobbly and misshapen. They came straight from oysters Gran had found on the beach, and they made Becca think of wet shoes, and the sea, and the mysterious things that go on inside oysters.

But Mum's pearls and Gran's had one thing in common: each one glistened with a moony shine.

"What do you do in the dark?" she asked Gran.

"Now that you're here, play Scrabble."

Becca set out the Scrabble. They played furiously. Outside, fog left its prints on the window, and the sounds of the sea hushed and receded.

"You can't do *poutine*!" Gran said. "It's not English. Not permitted."

"Well, there's no word that means *poutine* in English," Becca argued, "so I'm allowed to use it. *Poutine* is *poutine*. And look! It means I can use all my letters. And I can turn *ax* into *axe* on a triple word score."

"You can't use words that aren't English," Gran insisted. "And anyway you can say *poutine* in ordinary English — chips and cheese curds and gravy. It's just not one word."

"It's in the Scrabble dictionary," said Becca. "We looked it up once."

"The Scrabble dictionary!" Gran snorted. "In the good old days, we just used our brains. That's how I play, and that's the rule at my house. English words, and use your own brain."

Becca saw another word she could make somewhere else. *Pouting* she spelled, staring down at the board. Maybe this visit was going to be worse than she'd thought.

Gran went on to win by about a million points.

"See? Even if you'd got a bonus for using all your letters, I would have won," she said.

Becca packed up the game without saying a word.

"Well, it's time to go," Gran announced.

They were going out? It was coal-dark by now, and cold, too.

"Go where?"

"To get oysters. Get your boots on, Becca."

Gran threw the oyster shuckers and old oven mitts into her backpack.

"In the dark?"

"Yep."

A nasty Scrabble game and now Gran was taking her out into the woods in the dark and fog. It reminded Becca of a creepy fairy tale she'd read once.

"Hold my hand," said Gran's voice in the dark. "You don't want to trip."

"Can't we use flashlights?" Becca asked. "Why can't we get oysters from your beach?"

"We'll use the flashlight later. Your eyes won't get used to the dark if we use it now. And the fog gives its own light. We're going all the way to Mayfield Point because the beach out there has the best oyster beds. I hope you're feeling energetic. It's a long way."

"What's that smell?"

They stopped in the road and Gran sniffed.

"Trees' blood," Gran said. "Sap. Somebody is clearing to build a cabin."

Trees' blood. Becca shivered.

Mist drifted among the trees. Sometimes Becca could see trunks, and sometimes branches. She and Gran walked the trail to Mayfield Point in a glimmering haze, breathing water droplets lighter than the night.

"Do you hear that?" Gran stopped suddenly and pulled Becca still beside her.

Becca listened hard. It could have been the clouds, making a tiny patter on salal leaves.

"It's the sound of your own self," Gran told her. "It's the sound of your heart in your ears — your blood flowing."

Then Becca heard it, a rushing noise inside her own head, as if she had a moon-snail shell to her ear and was listening to its ocean rhythms. The sound of her own heart.

They walked on. The path curved through the forest toward the sea. Becca's feet told her she was walking uphill, and then that she was passing the tree with the eagles' nest.

"Are the eagles still here?" she asked, clutching Gran's hand.

"Yes, but their babies are teenagers now," Gran said. "Look, we're coming out on the beach."

But there was nothing to see, just fog all around. Becca felt pebbles underfoot and banged her shin on driftwood. She felt seaweed squish, and the crunch of oysters.

"Can't we use the flashlight?" she asked.

"In a minute."

Gran must see in the dark, Becca thought, stumbling beside her.

"Here's a good rock," Gran said, and she sat on it. "Yech! Soaked through already!"

Becca laughed.

"Okay! You bring me the oysters, and I'll shuck them," Gran directed.

"Where do you think they are now?" Becca asked.

"On the beach!"

"No, I mean Mum and Dad," Becca said. "Maybe they didn't go because of the fog."

"They're above the clouds, and we're right in them — the very same clouds. They're holding hands and saying, 'Becca's going to have a wonderful time with her old grandma. I hope they don't get up to no good!'" Gran paused. "Well, they don't really know we're out on the beach in the middle of the night. Now, where are those oysters?"

"Can I use the flashlight?"

"Oh, yes! Now's the time!"

"I thought you weren't supposed to eat oysters," Becca said.

"That's in summer," said Gran. "In February it's okay — more than okay! But we won't take many. Just enough for stew for the two of us and Frank."

Oyster stew. Ew. That, as well as totally unfair Scrabble rules and midnight walks.

Becca stomped off into the mist. It was so still that the sudden splash of her boots in the sea surprised her.

She stood in the water, looking down at her boots with the flashlight, and at the seaweed and snails and all the things that were so bright and clear in daylight. Now they looked weird and mysterious, as if they'd been caught by surprise in their secret night life.

Did snails sleep? Did oysters sleep? Did seaweed breathe out at night like trees and bushes did?

"I need oysters," Gran reminded her out of the dark.

Becca squelched on, shining the light down. Oysters lay loose on the beach. The shells had crusty frills that hurt her fingers.

"Can I do it?" she asked when she'd brought some oysters. "I've never done it before."

"Why not? Just be careful."

Gran gave Becca the oven mitts, now sloppy with oyster liquor. She showed her how to hold the oyster, and where to pry with the knife to break its muscle.

She put her strong hand over Becca's and helped her twist the shucker.

"There it goes!" Becca felt the shell give way.

"Your very first oyster," Gran said solemnly, suddenly not bossy at all.

"It has a frill inside, too."

"The mantle — that's how it sifts its food," Gran explained.

"It's soft! But what are these specks?" Becca ran her fingers over the cold, damp oyster and felt little hard bits — grit or bits of shell, she thought.

"Wait!" Gran shone the light on Becca's first oyster, and then she started to laugh. "Pearls!" she cried. "You've got a pearl — scads of pearls!"

"Really?" Becca was amazed, feeling the rolling bits with her fingers. "There's a whole bunch! My very own pearls."

"Careful!" Gran said. "You don't want to lose any. Here, you can put them in this."

She emptied the matchbox she kept in her backpack,

and Becca put the pearls in it, feeling carefully so she wouldn't miss any.

"You're certainly lucky, Rebecca my girl," Gran said. "You've found a whole handful of pearls all in one go. I can't believe it!"

Becca smiled and turned off the flashlight. The mist gave off a light of its own, and in her pocket was a match-box of pearls.

*   *   *

Later, she and Gran snuggled into Gran's Arctic sleeping bags down on the beach, and Frank curled up to sleep at her feet.

"That was some itchy oyster!" Gran said in wonder.

"Seventeen pearls," said Becca, for they had counted them together in the warmth of the cabin. "Seventeen!"

Becca could hear Gran smiling. A lopsided moon now shone through the mist, so that they lay in a pearly light themselves.

"And it's the same moon," said Becca.

"Yes. The same moon, shining down on us all," said Gran.

2. Herring

~~~~~~

"It's all very well living on an island, but you've got to have a boat," Gran declared. "And it's your last morning, so what better day for a sea voyage?"

Sixteen days had whizzed by. It had rained, it had blown and sometimes the sun had shone in a thin winterish way. Becca had piled more wood than she cared to remember. She had found out about the slippery algae that grew on the sandstone in winter. She still had the bruise from that discovery. She had counted widgeons and harlequins and pigeon guillemots for Gran's monthly bird count. Quite against her will she had taken lessons in how to turn compost. She had gone swimming although the water was polar. That had been an accident, too, and had only happened because Gran had asked her to wash vegetables in the sea. In the sea! What was wrong with the kitchen sink? But that was what chores were like at Gran's house. They involved the great outdoors.

Gran picked up the phone.

"Who are you calling?" Becca asked. "The boat shop?"

"No. I'm phoning Dugald. Ssssh!"

"Phoning Dugald" was how Gran described the local weather update. Now she listened carefully, not saying a word.

You didn't talk to the weather update. It talked to you. Sometimes the recording had a woman's voice; sometimes a man's. But it was always "phoning Dugald," because Dugald was the one with the nicest voice and the most interesting name. "Greetings," he would say, full of warmth and authority about weather. "This is Dugald blah-blah with the local weather update."

"What did he say?" Becca asked, hanging by her arms from the ladder that led to the loft where she slept.

"It wasn't him," said Gran. "But whoever it was said winds variable five to ten knots. High pressure system holding steady. A perfect day for the boat. Out!" she ordered, and Becca jumped off the ladder and hurried to pull on her boots.

At the boat shed Gran handed Becca life jackets and a pair of oars. She heaved the motor and gas tank into the wheelbarrow and trundled it down to the sea's edge.

"Where's the boat?" Becca asked. Gran's old boat, *Glaucous Gull*, was in "dry-docks" — overgrown with salal and green with algae and many seasons of congealed tree pollen.

"Under the cabin," Gran said. "I got a new one for myself for my birthday. New to me, I mean. It was second hand. A bargain!"

Under the cabin? Becca thought about how much

trouble she had squeezing under there during games of hide-and-seek with her cousins. What kind of boat could Gran store under there?

Gran wheeled the barrow back up the beach and hauled a huge duffel bag out from under the cabin.

"That's a boat?" Becca asked.

"It's a Zodiac."

Becca glanced up at the sky.

"Not the stars," Gran said. She heaved the duffel bag into the barrow and headed for the beach. "It's an inflatable boat, made in France."

Inflatable it might be, Becca thought, but as she and Gran struggled with its pieces and parts, it seemed more like one of those puzzles teachers give you to test your brain. Even the shapes of the boards were like a skill-testing question.

"I don't think we're too good at this," she said at last. The excitement of a voyage was getting lost in the bother of figuring out how to fit pieces of board into the Zodiac's floor — if that's what you called it. Maybe it was a deck.

"What do you mean?" Gran was holding a trapezoid-shaped board and trying to read the Zodiac manual at the same time. *"Montage,"* she read. "*Le volet avant... l'inter-section du fond et des flotteurs...*Where the — ?" she muttered. "If only I'd paid more attention in French. Now, where do these go? *Les longerons?*"

"They go along the side," Becca said.

"I thought you knew French," Gran said. "But you can't possibly be right about *les longerons*, so maybe you don't."

"It's the only place they *could* go!" Becca shouted.

"Hmph," said Gran. "If you shout at me you won't go anywhere, in or out of the Zodiac."

Do I really want to be stuck in a boat with her? Becca wondered.

Les longerons fit exactly where Becca had said. There was a sweaty session with the foot pump, gaskets and valve caps that didn't screw on quite as easily as they might have, and the fuss of fitting on the motor.

Gran tossed the foot pump and instruction manual into the floating Zodiac.

"I can't be bothered to take these back up to the cabin," she said. "We'll just take them along."

Even after all that trouble, Becca liked the Zodiac, with its inflated sides and bow. She had to sit on the bottom to row because there were no seats, but the oars were short enough for her to work properly. She rowed away from shore, hardly splashing at all.

What would her cousins Lucy and Alicia say if they could see her now? If they had been here, she would have had to argue for an hour to get a chance to row. That was one good thing about being with Gran on her own.

Gran let down the motor, adjusted the choke and pulled the starting cord.

"Have you done this before?" Becca asked, watching Gran's face go red.

Gran jerked the cord again.

"I beg your pardon?"

And again.

"I could keep rowing," Becca offered. This was even worse than arguing over Scrabble and turning compost.

Cough! Cough! Putt! Putt!

"Did you say something?" Gran asked, sitting up straight as a queen as she swung the tiller and headed them out to sea.

*   *   *

Over the side, Becca saw brown weed, sand through green water, the blackness of sand dollars. Then the bottom vanished.

When she looked up, Gran had steered them around the point.

"Where do you want to go?" Gran cried, zooming them over the March water, pale with the blue pale sky of spring.

"Let's go all the way around the island!" Becca shouted. "Hey, look! There's a kayak coming out of your bay!"

"Maybe it's the tree-chopping man, the guy clearing for a cabin," Gran hollered over the buzzing motor. "Okay, then, let's rip!"

Becca lay against the side of the Zodiac. Seawater splattered into her hair. The kayak near Gran's bay became a speck in the distance as the Zodiac skimmed southward, hopping ripples.

"Look, another helicopter," Becca called. "That's the third one I've seen."

"Maybe the pilots are practicing!"

There went Bouldings' cabin. There went Mayfield

Point. Past Camas Island and its light. Past the sea-lion rocks — now, for some reason, empty of sea lions.

"We used to row here when your mother was little," Gran said, "in the days before we went modern." She patted the motor. "Now that was a long day."

"Can I drive?" Becca asked suddenly.

It didn't look so hard.

"I guess you can give it a go."

Gran showed Becca how to turn the handle to speed up and slow down, how to push the tiller to steer and where to attach the safety clip to her life jacket.

Then she sat beside her while Becca steered along beside the cliffs.

"Usually there are cormorants all over these cliffs," Gran said.

Another helicopter clattered over, and Becca motored across the mouth of Admiral's Bay toward Sandy Point.

"I wouldn't mind going a bit faster!" she said.

She sat up on her knees to see what was coming. Only sea, shore and trees, she supposed, and the snowy mountains of Vancouver Island. The blue and gold and green of a sunny day on Gran's island.

She turned the control, and the Zodiac shot around Sandy Point like a creature running for its life.

* * *

But it was a creature running *into* life. It burst into the sound of a million gulls, the blur of thousands of seabirds hovering like a noisy cloud above the water.

"Not just gulls," Gran cried. "There's an osprey! And eagles!"

"And look!" Becca had seen Gran's sea many colors, but never like this. It looked like milk had spilled into its blue — and what blue! Turquoise, aquamarine, azure — there wasn't a word for this kind of blue.

"What is it?" Becca screamed over the sound of the gulls and the motor.

"Milt!" Gran was kneeling right up at the bow, tugging frantically at her binoculars in the backpack.

"Milk? Why milk?"

"Not milk — MILT!" Gran startled Becca by grinning hugely. "Herring, Becca!"

The Zodiac bounded across the water with great leaps. Becca sat down hard on the bottom boards, clutching the tiller.

It wasn't just birds screaming with frenzy that she had to look out for. Hundreds of boats were out — trawlers, skiffs, runabouts, Coast Guard and Fisheries ships. Seaplanes and helicopters buzzed overhead, whining like crazed seabirds themselves.

"What are they doing?" Becca shouted.

"They're waiting to hear if the herring are ripe!"

"Right? Right about what?"

"Not right — RIPE," shouted Gran.

What would make herring ripe, Becca wondered — unless, of course, you were talking about smell. Kippered herring, rollmops... yech.

"Cut the motor!" Gran yelled.

"What do you mean, ripe? What's going on?"

"This time of year the herring come to spawn! They lay their eggs in the seaweed and then the babies hatch and you can see them break out and swim away. Just like little ghost fish! Transparent! Be careful where you're going! Look out for that sea lion!"

Gran cowered and shielded her head. A great swoosh of sea almost swamped them.

With all the seals and sea lions breeching and diving, the Zodiac pitched and bucked. Sea lions' urgent barking, gulls' skirling, the weird, high laughter of eagles and the helicopters' clatter filled Becca's ears. Tails slapped. Beaks ripped and tore and sliced. Eagles stretched out knife-sharp talons and raked up their prey. Water streamed as seals and sea lions dove and surfaced, exploding out of the water with their mouths bristling with fish.

"The fishermen aren't allowed to start fishing until the herring are actually laying their eggs — when they're ripe," Gran hollered, her binoculars trained on ospreys and eagles. "That's why everyone's hanging about here. They're waiting for the Fisheries people to tell them they can start!"

"The sea lions aren't waiting!" Becca yelled, pushing the tiller hard over to dodge a fat seal.

Gran didn't seem to hear her. Gulls flapped madly, splashed down and lifted themselves out, gullets stopped with herring. Wheeling and crying, beaks open, tongues stiff with noise-making — wings beat, throats vibrated.

Becca's brain buzzed. Her arm burned with the effort

of holding the boat steady. The sea was full of burbling foam and shifting colors. Seals and sea lions hurled themselves around in careless frenzy and the boat heaved with the surges of their diving. Becca had to duck as an eagle whooshed right over her, so close that she could see its yellow eye, its hooked beak, and feel the wind of its flight in her hair.

"Bonapartes," Gran hollered. "Immature glaucous-winged. Look, there's another osprey, and another one. Is that a common tern? Mergansers. Harlequins. And here are the cormorants, look! Ow!"

Great lumps of sea hit Becca in the side of her head.

"We're going to sink!" she yelled. "A sea lion might land on us! It's so loud! And wet! It's time to go!"

Suddenly, Gran was there with Becca. She cut the motor.

"We'll just drift! That won't be so scary."

"Drift! We're going to be swamped!"

The hurly-burly of millions of seabirds and fish and sea mammals and boats made the Zodiac heave and tremble like a helpless herring itself.

The sea was black with fish. Dark backs turned to Becca, so many she couldn't see past them, rank after rank, belly to back, flank to flank.

"It looks like the sea's growing fur," she yelled, leaning on the side of the Zodiac. Herring fins poked out of the water everywhere. They speared up like newly sprung grass, like a dark lawn.

The boat lurched suddenly.

"Don't fall in!" Gran shouted. "We'll never get the stink out of you! They call it finning when they gather like this!"

Becca hung on to the edge of the Zodiac for dear life. She lay on the *flotteur* to peer into the water. It molded itself around her as if it were protecting her from the teeth and jaws of creatures at home in the sea.

"Laying eggs is an agitated business," Gran said.

She spoke with such certainty that Becca thought maybe she'd actually laid eggs herself.

The side of the Zodiac was really quite comfortable, if only the greedy seals and sea lions wouldn't keep heaving the sea around and threatening to whack her with their tails.

Slosh! There they went again, pitching from the force of another attacking sea lion. The side squished around Becca and her face almost dipped into the sea.

In a moment, in the space of a breath, a wet whiskered face thrust into hers. Pinched nostrils and wide eyes, fur so wet — so real! — and so close! And herring in its mouth, staring up at her!

Becca shrieked. Her head tipped into the sea, herring and all.

The seal vanished.

"Gran!"

Becca's heart pounded. The floor of the Zodiac buckled, Gran said, "Dear me, I think we've sprung a leak," and from somewhere nearby a man said, "Can I help you?"

Everything happened at once.

"Help!" Becca scrambled away from the side. "We're sinking! We're going to drown! That seal smelled!"

"What? What are you hollering about?" shouted Gran. "You're not going to drown! But what's happening to our boat?"

"Can I help you?" Becca heard again, and at the same time she saw that parts of the Zodiac sagged. A *chambre flottante* sighed and collapsed before her eyes.

"We've got the pump," she said, wiping her herringy face. She didn't want to end up among the seals and sea lions. "Quick! We have to get out of here! Did you see that seal? It practically attacked me!"

"It was probably just curious," Gran told her. "Look at that eagle! It must have thirty fish in its beak!"

Becca didn't know what to do. The foot pump was there, but she didn't see how she could use it. The floorboards were too loose to stand on and anyway, you weren't supposed to stand up in a boat. Gran was watching eagles, not even thinking about how to get a flabby Zodiac out of danger. Even now the boat's droopy side tilted toward the sea. Water sloshed over it and right there, all around them, wild creatures gorged and argued, snatched and tore with no care for Becca or Gran or their limp little boat.

"Gran?!"

"Excuse me." Again Becca heard the friendly voice. It was the man in the kayak. "Are you having trouble?" he asked.

"How do you do?" Gran said, lowering her binoculars. "Can I help you?"

"Actually, I was wondering if I could help you," the man said. "I don't suppose you have a pump with you...?"

"We do," Becca said quickly. She rummaged under the backpacks and extra life jackets until she found it. Her hair was dripping from her unexpected face wash. Her heart was thumping too hard.

Mr. Kayak paddled around to the valve nearest Becca and unscrewed it.

"It's a new boat," Becca told him. "It can't have a leak."

"This is new?" asked Mr. Kayak.

"New to us. Second hand, really."

"Well, it may not have a real leak," he said. "Maybe you got something stuck in the valve. It isn't screwed on properly. Hey!" He had to clutch on to the side as a seal surfaced right by his kayak.

"Maybe there's a problem with the *capet et buchon*," Gran suggested. "Or the *membrane fixé*."

Now that she'd made her contribution, Gran went back to her binoculars — as though nothing was wrong with the boat at all, as though they were not in danger of slithering in among herring and seals, terrifying sea lions and birds berserk with plenty.

"There's a problem with the gasket," Mr. Kayak said, looking at Gran with wonder. "Not the *membrane fixé* — although that's got old seaweed on it, which isn't too swift. Never mind, I've cleaned it off. This is a very mature new boat, if you don't mind my saying so. The gasket — anybody got any gum?"

"Would soggy Kleenex do?" Becca asked. "I mean, it's just seawater, not, you know — "

Mr. Kayak didn't seem to mind the damp tissue. He stuck a bit in the leaky valve. "There, that should fix the seal for now. Where's the pump?"

"How are you going to work it?"

"Special exercises," Mr. Kayak said. He fit the nozzle into the valve. "By the way, how do you do? My name's Macallan. Mac for short. What's yours? You look about the same age as someone I know. Whoops!"

Another sudden tilt almost had Becca and Mac tipped into the sea.

"Help! Becca. And Gran's Isobel. She's …"

She didn't know quite what to say.

"She doesn't have a strong sense of self-preservation?" asked Mac. "Why isn't she terrified? Or a little anxious, at least?"

"How do you do?" Gran said abruptly, swinging her binoculars to take in Mac.

"Pleased to meet you. Bird dung is a real hazard," he replied, and wiped his arm. "Although in some cultures, getting pooped on is considered fortunate. And now — "

He held the foot pump between his hands and squeezed. Muscles jumped in his chest. Becca could see them moving under his T-shirt. The pump snorted and gusted rhythmically, one-two-three.

"It's kind of you to help us," Gran said, finally paying attention to something besides wildlife. "Thank you."

Becca prodded the side of the Zodiac. It was already firmer.

"What if we'd sunk!" she exclaimed.

"Well," said Gran, "there are two other *chambres flottantes* intact. That's why I didn't let it distract me from what's important!"

What could be more important than staying alive? Becca didn't think the two other air chambers would have saved them. Even now a fisherman was zooming right near them, his wake splattering into the boat. If Mac hadn't pumped up that side, they'd be swimming right now.

If she hadn't been stuck in the boat with Gran, Becca would have stomped off.

Mac screwed the cap on the valve, clutching at the Zodiac to keep himself steady.

"You'll have to fix it properly," he said like a boat doctor, "but that should last until you get home. Not that I know anything about boats, of course."

"They're going nuts!" Becca exclaimed, as a sea lion choked on its enormous mouthful.

Gran lowered the binoculars and smiled.

"Be careful in that kayak," she said to Mac. "Winds variable, five to ten knots."

Mac laughed. "Right-o," he agreed. "It's a nice day. If you're into zoological turbulence."

He saluted with his paddle and moved away.

"I'm sure I've met that man before," Gran said, looking after him. "His voice sounds familiar. And what a wonderful name! Macallan is one of my favorite single malts."

"What's single malt? My hair's all wet," Becca said. "My face tastes of herring. Do you think that seal was trying to kiss me or bite my head off?"

"Let's say it kissed you," she said, putting her binoculars away at last. "And we should go now, I think. It's going to get dark and we don't have lights."

"I don't want to go," Becca said. It was the last afternoon of her seventeen days. Now that they had drifted to the margins of the herring madness, she didn't want to leave the sea, or the hollering birds, or the eggs that Gran said would hatch like little ghost fish. She didn't want to leave the Zodiac, or even Gran herself.

But she steered them back around Sandy Point. Clamor and clatter were suddenly silenced and she headed past sandstone cliffs, across Admiral's Bay, past Camas Island light.

"The seals will probably be too stuffed to swim back here tonight," she said. "Their mums will be up with them in the night."

She steered, and as she watched the island slip past, she thought. She thought about the seventeen pearls she had found in the moonlight, and Frank looking out of the fog, and her boots filled with seawater. She thought of swimming in March, and flying over the sea in the Zodiac. She thought of Mac's muscles jumping as he pumped up the Zodiac, and the smell of trees' blood, and the sound of her own blood rushing in her ears.

There had been no Mum and Dad, no aunts or cousins or friends. It had just been Becca and Gran for seventeen days, and none of it had been sad or boring. Annoying sometimes, but never dull.

She headed the Zodiac into Gran's bay. The setting sun flashed, reflected from windows on cabins across the water. Gran moved to the stern and turned off the motor. The Zodiac drifted up to the sandstone in the twilight, and Becca dipped her hand in the cold sea.

"If you count my pearls as days, this is the last one," Becca said. "But if you count them as adventures, I still have lots to go."

3. The Hike

~~~~~~

WHEN Becca returned to Gran's island in May, she came with Dad and her cousins Lucy and Alicia.

"I have too much to do before summer," said Mum, kissing her goodbye. "I'll come then. I love you."

Becca made the I-love-you sign with her fingers and Dad drove away.

"No way am I spending the whole weekend sweating in a garden," Lucy declared as soon as she got in the car.

"Life is too short," Alicia agreed.

Becca sighed.

Alicia was fourteen and Lucy was twelve. Becca admired how definite they were, but she couldn't help hoping that Mac would be around, or someone, anyway, who would be better company than her cousins. She imagined someone certain but not bossy. A person who had good ideas for excursions, but who didn't mind listening to someone else once in a while. A friend.

On the other hand, Lucy and Alicia could help turn the compost.

"I mean, I don't mind digging for a while but this is supposed to be a holiday," Lucy went on.

"There are lots of other things to do," Becca reminded them.

"We know," Alicia said. "We've been going there longer than you."

Maybe, Becca thought. But you've never found seventeen pearls.

She thought about her pearls as Dad drove them on to the first ferry, and the second ferry, and the third ferry. And when they arrived there was Gran, threatening to serve them kippered herring for dinner because it was Frank's favorite.

*　　*　　*

Frank came up to the communal garden with them the next morning. Gran opened the deer gate, Frank strutted through and everyone followed him.

"Never leave the gate open," Gran warned, pushing it closed. "The deer would eat everything in sight and my neighbors would have fits."

"I know!" said Lucy and Alicia, as if they were one person.

The garden was an oasis in a field of sedge and brambles. All the neighbors had their own plots and the whole area was fenced with barbed wire, criss-crossed wire and netting to keep deer out.

"The Keswicks' sweetpeas are already up to my knees," Lucy said.

"Oh, you know them," Gran said. "They live for gardening!"

Nobody could accuse Gran of living for gardening. That was one of the reasons she got the family to dig for her.

"Look!" Alicia pointed. "Kay's tomatoes already have flowers on them, and yours aren't even planted."

"Hey!" said Gran. "What are you? The garden report squad? My lavender is doing well. And look at the rosemary. It's huge!"

Those two herbs were the only plants Becca recognized in the sea of grass, weeds and winter-deadened sticks that was Gran's allotment.

"You've got some very robust thistles," Dad said. "Don't forget them!"

He was grinding his teeth, Becca noticed.

"It's very tasty rosemary!" Gran said, looking miffed.

"Rosemary!" snorted Dad.

"Next year we could come in winter and cover it all with seaweed," Becca said. "That's what Kay does. It keeps the grass and weeds down, she says. She calls it putting the garden to bed. Then you'd have lavender and rosemary and flowers and veg, too."

"Seaweed!" exclaimed Gran. "All that salt! Terrible for the garden! Don't even mention it!"

But Becca couldn't help noticing Kay's terrifically happy-looking flowers and vegetables. They didn't look like the seaweed had hurt them at all.

"Where do we start?" she asked.

"Here." Lucy pointed to the earth by Becca's feet.

"Inch by inch. Or centimeter by centimeter, if you prefer." She sighed importantly. "It's like this every year, isn't it, Uncle Hill?"

She jammed her fork into the wilderness.

Becca poked her own fork into the hard ground. Lucy and Alicia were right about one thing at least. It was tough work.

*   *   *

The heat of the May sun bloomed around them, and bit by bit, the green mat of spring weeds changed to the damp brown of turned earth. Becca's palms became red and hot from digging, and sweat dripped into her eyes.

"You girls have made such great progress that I might give you part of the afternoon off," Dad said as they ate cheese and oatcakes and chocolate, sprawled around the gardening tools, the water barrels and the wheelbarrow.

"All I want is to go for a swim," Alicia groaned.

"Me, too!" Becca couldn't wait to jump into the sea.

"Maybe in a couple of hours," Dad said. "If we get the whole plot turned over, we'll take a break and then plant tomorrow."

"It's a deal!" Lucy and Alicia cried together.

Becca saw them exchange a look. She knew that look. Something was up. They had a plan.

*   *   *

"Yes, Becca is going with you."

Gran probably meant to speak softly, but Becca heard her anyway.

"But, Gran — "

"And there will be no nonsense," Gran ordered.

Silence. Becca made sure to thump up the back steps so Gran would know she was there. How embarrassing. But why shouldn't Lucy and Alicia include her? Besides, if she didn't go with them she'd be alone or once again stuck with adults.

"I hung up the suits," she announced.

"I didn't know you could reach the clothesline," Alicia said.

How did she make such an ordinary comment sound so mean?

"I stood on the chopping block."

"Are you ready to go?" Lucy asked.

Becca knew Lucy hoped she would say no.

"Sure," she said. "What are we waiting for?"

*   *   *

"You won't be able to come if you don't keep up," Alicia said sternly over her shoulder. For some reason she was carrying a thick coil of rope, but that didn't slow her down.

"She isn't trying to be nasty," Lucy explained, walking backwards so she could face Becca. "It's just that there's a certain place we want to go, and if we don't hurry there won't be time."

The smell from Mac's chopping and sawing lingered even though Mac wasn't there. Becca saw the clean wood of a new house frame rising among the trees, and a glint of red from the belly of the kayak. She thought of telling Lucy and Alicia about how she and Gran had nearly sunk the Zodiac.

"Hurry up!" Lucy wailed over her shoulder, and Becca knew they couldn't care less about the Zodiac or even about her being kissed by a seal.

Alicia leaped the ditch and headed off through the bracken at the edge of the forest.

So they weren't going to the park.

"Where are we going?"

Lucy started to run.

"Come on!"

Lucy jumped.

Becca jumped.

Cedars and bracken gave way to salal, to hemlock and Douglas fir. Becca heard Lucy and Alicia rustling through the bush ahead of her.

"Is there a path here?" Becca called.

Nobody answered.

Glossy leaves spread before her. Above the leaves, pale salal blossoms nodded on red stems like round little ghosts of the berries they would be in summer. Becca pushed against the bushes with her arms and chest, and tough, snaky stems caught at her feet. Leaves scratching on her clothes and the sound of her own breathing filled her ears.

"Lucy! Alicia!"

A faint murmur drifted back to her, and then she heard a crunching sound.

"What? What do you want?" demanded Alicia, suddenly standing beside her.

"I didn't know where you were," Becca said.

"You're going to have to keep up," Alicia told her. "I knew we shouldn't have let you come. If you get lost, don't blame me. Now come on."

After a while branches were whipping Becca's face. She was climbing over fallen trees, and when she looked up, she saw only leaves and branches. It was easier to tunnel under the salal and weasel through the stalks. But she had no idea where she was going. The soles of Lucy's runners and her faded cutoffs were the only landmarks, and they were always disappearing into the shadowy bush ahead of her.

"Are you sure this is the right way?" Becca heard Lucy ask.

She didn't hear the answer.

A while later she almost bumped into Alicia.

"There!" Alicia said triumphantly. "There's that tree! We have to head over there."

"What tree?" Lucy was grumpy. "There are thousands of trees. Millions!"

Becca couldn't see any trees at all, just the underside of salal leaves. But Alicia and Lucy had already crunched off and she had to scramble to keep the back of them in sight.

The next time she bumped into them they were sitting on a fallen log, still surrounded by a sea of salal and Douglas fir.

"You always get us lost," Lucy argued. "Why don't you let me go first for a change?"

"We're not lost," Alicia insisted. "We're just in the woods."

"Yeah, but where in the woods?"

It was green and cool resting there under the salal in the middle of the forest. Becca closed her eyes and listened to her cousins argue.

When she opened them, it was because something wet and cold had touched her face.

Frank's nose.

"Frank!" she whispered. "What are you doing here?"

His white feet twinkled, his black tail swished, and Becca crawled through the bush after him.

"I'm going," she said loudly. "You can follow me if you want."

But she was making so much noise going in and out of the salal stalks that she couldn't tell whether her cousins were behind her or not.

"Are you looking for mice?" she asked Frank.

But Frank just moved steadily through the bush.

"The salal's not so thick," she mentioned to him. "It's getting lighter."

Now Becca could hear Lucy and Alicia behind her, scrambling to keep up.

"Does she know where she's going?" she heard Alicia ask.

"I don't know, but it can't be any worse than following you around," Lucy retorted.

Becca smiled. In a moment, her head poked out of the salal altogether.

She was on the edge of a silver forest.

"Frank?" she called.

Frank had vanished, but in front of her oak trees rose up like spindly pillars, shaking tufts of leaves on the ends of high, gnarled limbs. The leaves looked like so many hands waving to the world. The sun lit up the rough tree bark and it shone silver and gray. The whole glade smelled mossy and sweet, and the grasses were starred with wildflowers — blue and yellow and white.

Becca had never seen anything like it.

"It's a magic place," she said out loud.

The trees whispered with their leaves.

"I'll make a wish," she said, and she put her arms around one of the oaks and spoke quietly into its rough, warm bark.

"What are you doing?" Alicia demanded.

She and Lucy were standing at the edge of the salal, watching Becca curiously.

"What I want," she said, still holding the tree.

"Where are we?" Lucy began, but as she looked around she, too, was overtaken by the spell of the silvery old trees. She walked among them and touched them as Becca had done.

"This isn't where I wanted to go," Alicia said.

Becca hardly heard her. If I had a friend, she thought, I could come here with her. Lucy and Alicia would never know. Frank could bring us, or I could even find my own way.

"Where were you trying to go?" she asked.

"To the store!" answered Alicia. "But how do we get there from here?"

"It was your big idea," said Lucy. "You should know the way."

Becca looked across the sea. There was Sandy Point. She recognized the shape of its hill from passing it on the day of the herring. Beyond that were the snowy peaks of Vancouver Island.

Well. Now she knew where they were. Follow the shore one way, and they'd get back to Gran's. Follow it the other way, and they'd get to the store. Eventually.

"I know it's possible," Alicia said. "If you look at a map you can see — "

"We can do it," Becca agreed. "It's just that — "

"Well, what are we waiting for?" Alicia asked. "Let's go!"

*   *   *

"It's a long way," Becca said later.

Bits of tree were stuck in her hair, and her feet were all sweaty inside her shoes. She couldn't think of anything but how good it would be to feel cold seawater on her hot skin.

"It's not so bad," said Alicia scornfully. She was rude again now that she thought she knew the way. And her legs were longer.

"You can have ice cream when we get there," Lucy promised.

"I didn't bring my allowance," Becca said.

"I'll get yours," Lucy offered. "After all, if it weren't for you we'd probably still be lost. How many days do you think this is going to take?" she asked Alicia.

"Look! It's opening out now," Alicia said. "We can get down here and walk the rest of the way on the beach."

I don't think so, Becca thought, peering over the edge of a cliff.

"It's only a little cliff," said Alicia. "It's what I brought the rope for."

"Yeah, it's really little," Lucy said.

"Don't be a drip," retorted Alicia. "It's not that far. It isn't any higher than Gran's loft."

"Which you fell out of and broke your arm last year," said Lucy. "And anyway, this is higher. Lots higher."

"Lucy's right," Becca said quickly, gazing down through the trees to where the ground dropped off a long way above the beach.

"It's no big deal," scoffed Alicia. "There's tons of good footholds."

"Oh, sure," Lucy said.

Becca braced herself on the hillside, hanging on to a branch so she wouldn't slide over the edge. How would she end up, if she slipped? Cuts and abrasions, like the Band-Aid box said. Crushed and bleeding, probably. A few broken bones. And worse.

"How are we supposed to get down?" she asked.

"The rope!" said Alicia. "I learned these cool knots. They're just right for this kind of thing. A bowline! A sheepshank! A clove-hitch! We'll tie you up in the rope and let you down, because you're littlest, and then Lucy and I will climb down ourselves hanging on to the rope."

Becca looked at Lucy.

"I don't have a clue," Lucy whispered. "But eat whatever you have in your pockets. It could be your last meal."

*   *   *

Becca was knotted into Alicia's bowline, but it didn't make her feel any better. She stood at the top of the cliff and looked at the stones below. Some were covered with barnacles, and some with seaweed.

"Are you sure this is a good idea?" she asked. Why had she even wanted to come along on this expedition? She couldn't remember.

"Come on, Becca," said Alicia briskly. "It's getting late and the store might close."

"The store doesn't have anything I want to die for," Becca said, looking down.

Alicia ignored her.

"I'll treat you, and Lucy will, too. Double junk food. Here, I'll hold the rope tight around the tree and let you down slowly. Use your feet and hands. Like you're climbing, only down instead of up, and with a safety line."

Safety? Was that the right word?

Becca hoped so. She took a deep breath and rolled over so her legs were hanging down. Already she could feel Alicia's rope sneaking up her ribs.

"What if I fall out of it?"

"You won't," Alicia said cheerfully. "Go on! Squinch backwards. I'll let you down slowly."

Becca had a great view of Alicia's scabby knees and scratched shins. How fascinating, she thought. Alicia has a mole on her left leg and her ratty-looking socks are stuck full of burrs.

That was before the sandstone began to scratch into her stomach and part of her shirt decided to stay somewhere farther up the cliff.

"Ow!" Becca yelled as the rope bit under her arms.

"Hang on to the line, you dodo!" Alicia shouted. "Think of ice cream! Licorice shoelaces!"

"I hate licorice," Becca yelled. "And don't call me names!"

Her stomach was probably bleeding. Her shirt was rucked up to her armpits. She could feel knobs and ledges in the rock with her feet, but not see them. Her knees kept banging into the stone. Soon they would look worse than Alicia's and they would hurt more, too.

"How much do you weigh, anyway?" Alicia suddenly asked, rather out of breath.

"Don't let go!" Becca said.

She swung around on the rope, eyeing the rocks below.

"Can't you get a good foothold?" Alicia called. "Caramels. Jelly beans. Chips."

Becca was halfway there.

"What are you doing?" demanded Alicia.

"Can't I even rest for one second?" Becca grumbled.

There was a sudden shower of earth and dead leaves, right down on her head. She heard Lucy yelp.

"What are you doing?" she yelled.

"The rope is kind of slipping," said Alicia calmly. "And Lucy almost fell off the cliff. Hurry up."

Becca's nose scraped against rock. She could see every grain of sand in the sandstone, every chip and crack. She'd never noticed before how many shades of brown and pink and yellow and orange could be in one piece of rock.

Bang! With a meter to go the rope broke and she fell on to the stones, her foot stuck between two of them and her calf bleeding from barnacle scrapes. Nothing too serious, and now she could look forward to food. Suddenly, she could hear her stomach growling.

It was too bad it took Lucy and Alicia so long to get down the cliff themselves. It wasn't nearly as easy as Alicia had said, and she was stuck for a long time trying to get past the overhang. Because the rope had broken off short, she and Lucy had to make a little jump from up the cliff on to the rocks, which were big and lumpy and a perfect place to break bones.

When Alicia finally made it to solid ground she had to sit still for quite a while.

"It feels late," Lucy observed as they hiked across Admiral's Bay. "I hope the store's still open. I'm starved!"

*   *   *

"A meat pie and a carton of milk," Lucy said as they pushed open the door of the store, which was still hopping even though it was almost closing time. "What do you want, Becca?"

A meat pie! And then a banana. A bottle of ginger beer, which she liked and nobody else did, so they wouldn't ask her to share. Some cookies and a bag of chips. It would be a feast — almost a midnight feast. Well, that wasn't really true, but it felt like it.

"I need that shipment of pipes by Wednesday," a man was telling Mrs. Barker, the cashier. "There's a new place out on Bosun's Bay I'm going to be plumbing."

"Don't worry, Merlin. The guys down in hardware say it'll be here by then," Mrs. Barker said, and the pipe man scooped up his groceries and headed out the door. "Next?"

Alicia dumped her pile of groceries on the counter.

"That'll be $22.47," said Mrs. Barker.

Lucy reached into her pocket, and Alicia reached into hers. Becca knew they had fifteen dollars each, but she saw the same look of horror pass over both their faces at the same time.

"I changed my shorts," they said.

"What?"

"The money's in my other shorts," they said, in perfect unison.

Becca had never seen them look so crushed, and it didn't help that her stomach began to growl so ferociously that even Mrs. Barker gave her a look.

But at that very moment, she heard a familiar voice.

"Mac!" she said.

"Becca! I didn't know you were here for the holiday."

"It's not a holiday, really, just planting Gran's garden," she said. "Are you working on your cabin?"

"I just got here and tomorrow I'll do just that," Mac said. "How's your gran? Any shipwrecks or drownings recently? Any displays of affection between you and the local marine life?"

"No. We've just been digging and digging! But could you give me and my cousins a ride home?"

Alicia was glaring at her, partly in admiration, but there was something else, too. She wanted Becca to borrow money. Becca pretended not to see her, even though she was starving.

"Cousins!" exclaimed Mac. "So that's who they are. Sure, I'll give you a lift. Here — give your gran a call on my cell and I'll be ready in a second."

That was how Mac rescued them, sort of — and even though they were a lot earlier than they would have been if they'd had to go home on foot, it was long past dinnertime when they walked into the cabin.

There, with a terrible hunger burning and gnawing in their stomachs and the soles of their feet buzzing with weariness, they had to face Dad and Gran. Words such as "cockamamie," "half baked" and "peril" sizzled in the air, along with "grounded" and "what would I tell your mum if you fell over the cliff?" After that even Alicia didn't complain about the truly awful meal of scrambled eggs and cold stir-fried lamb's-quarters, made of weeds Gran had harvested from the beach.

"So many of your expeditions just seem to go on and on," Becca heard Lucy say to Alicia as they burrowed into sleeping bags at last. "And then we end up without decent food and getting into trouble, too!"

Becca looked down at the scrapes on her stomach and the places the rope had rubbed her skin raw. They were a sign that adventures were out there even if they didn't always end gloriously.

And she thought of something else. Lucy and Alicia were ornery, but they did make things happen.

And if they could make things happen, she could, too.

4. Blackberries

~~~~~~

BECCA thought about adventures off and on as she finished up the school year, and Sports Day, and watched her mum get big. So big, in fact, that when it was time to head to Gran's for the usual August visit, Mum and Dad didn't dare come.

"It's a bit too close to the time," Mum said. "But you can go. You'll have a good time and Gran will love it."

"Gran will not love it," said Becca. "She'll argue about Scrabble and get me to do a lot of chores and tell me not to flush the toilet because it wastes water."

Two days later she left with Aunt Fifi, who was actually quite good at making things happen.

"Look at all the jellyfish," she said as they leaned over the rail of the ferry. "That usually means the water is cold."

Aunt Fifi loved cold water. She loved it more than Gran did, even.

"First swim, then blackberries," she told Becca. "I want to make jelly."

Aunt Fifi was always full of projects. Becca turned her face to the wind and watched the island come closer.

*   *   *

"Are the blackberries ripe?" Aunt Fifi asked after she'd bounded up the ferry ramp and hugged Gran.

"Ripe, luscious and dropping from the bushes," Gran answered. "If you care to risk your life for them. Becca, stop climbing on that rail."

"Risk her life?" Becca asked. "I'm fine on the rail." Was Gran going to be all bossy again?

"Girl in the red jacket, stop climbing on the guard rail," boomed the ferry's P.A. system. "It is against ferry regulations to climb on ferry property."

Becca leaped to the ground feeling as red as her jacket.

"Hey! You could have told me," she said to Gran.

"I mean the blackberry bushes are like Sleeping Beauty's hedge," Gran replied. "I did tell you to get off the rail. Now, let me take a look at you... A little taller, a little frecklier, that's what I like to see. How's your mum?"

"Huge," Becca said, thinking of the bulge that was going to be a sister or brother.

"It won't be long now," Gran said.

*   *   *

They ate bowls of Gran's scary soup for dinner, sitting on the beach. Frank crouched at Becca's feet and looked at her hopefully.

"Can't I give him some?" Becca asked. Whoever had told Gran that sea asparagus made good soup should be — actually, Becca didn't know what a proper punishment might be, except maybe that they should have to eat it every day for a year. And not be allowed to floss.

"Absolutely not," said Gran. "Sit down, Fiona. You're spilling soup all over creation."

But Aunt Fifi stood up to eat, gazing out to sea and pacing the sandstone in between bouts of picking sea asparagus fibers from between her teeth. She didn't look as though she thought spilling her soup would be a great tragedy.

"I'll just run over and check on the blackberries myself," she said suddenly. "If you're right, we'll go tomorrow. Right after breakfast."

"Oh, for goodness' sake, Fiona," said Gran. "I already told you they're ripe. Can't you sit still even for a minute?"

"Absolutely not," said Aunt Fifi. "Want to go swimming when I get back, Becca?"

*   *   *

In the morning Gran refused to go with them.

"I'm waiting for the plumber to phone," she said. "You know how that is. If I miss the call, I won't get to speak to him for a week."

Gran had a complicated system of rainwater cisterns that fed into her indoor plumbing, and she had to consult frequently with a whole team of pipe and pump people.

"My mother has an interesting relationship with the plumber," Aunt Fifi told Becca.

"He has big feet and holes in his jeans," Becca said. That's all she'd ever seen of him.

"He very well may," said Aunt Fifi. "All I know is that his opinions on English literature are absurd."

Last summer Becca had heard Aunt Fifi and the plumber have a terrible argument about one of Shakespeare's sonnets. The plumber had had his head under the house at the time, but Becca had seen his feet twitching violently, as if they were having the argument themselves. Gran had been upset when he left before he had finished the job. He'd had to come back another day when Aunt Fifi wasn't there.

"Are we taking the ladder?" Becca asked, changing the topic.

"Yes," said Aunt Fifi. "And you'd better change your clothes. Shorts and a T-shirt are no good for brambles. Gum boots, long sleeves and jeans are fit attire."

Fit attire, Becca thought. Sometimes it was like Aunt Fifi was teaching a university course no matter where she was.

"It's boiling hot out," Becca said. "I'm not wearing jeans."

"You absolutely must!" Aunt Fifi insisted. "Look at me! And if it weren't so hard to pick with gloves on I'd wear them, too. I'm an expert! You should take my advice."

"Bossing" was what Becca called it. But she saw that she'd have to give in a little.

"Well, all right," she said at last. "I'll wear gum boots but I won't wear jeans or long sleeves."

"You'll be sorry!" Aunt Fifi predicted.

*　　*　　*

Becca and Aunt Fifi clanked off. The handle of the bucket bit into Becca's arm and the end of the ladder dug into her fingers. Aunt Fifi rattled with buckets and plastic containers, all strung on what she called her special blackberry-picking stick.

"You'll need one, too," she said. "To pull down the high branches."

"How many are we going to pick?" Becca asked.

"Lots! Oceans of them. I want enough jelly to last for years."

"How far is it?" Becca asked.

"Not too far," Aunt Fifi told her. "You won't even have time to get blisters."

Walking down the road wasn't so bad, but it was a tight squeeze through the fence into the deserted farmstead.

"The best berries grow here," Aunt Fifi explained, pulling at the barbed wire until it creaked. "The fattest ones are along the fence on the other side," she said, inspecting a barbed-wire tear in her shirt.

"Aren't you hot?" Becca asked. She was ready for a swim and they hadn't even begun to pick yet. The field, overgrown with grass now dry and gone to seed, seemed vast. Grass seeds dropped into her boots and made her ankles itch.

"A little," said Aunt Fifi, "but at least I won't get scratched to bits, like some people."

Blackberries drooped from the bushes in great clusters, just as luscious and plentiful as Gran had said. Becca stood in the shadow of the brambles and let berries fall into her hand, and then into the pot.

"I love picking blackberries," said Aunt Fifi from up the ladder. "It's so peaceful."

It sure was peaceful, Becca thought. Boring, even. *Plump, plump, plump.* The berries dropped into the bucket. The only other sound was from bees in late blossoms, and the quiet noises of a calm sea.

"What did you and the plumber argue about?" Becca asked.

"Are you trying to stir things up?" demanded Aunt Fifi. "Ow. I scratched myself."

"I just wondered." They had to talk about something. It was dull to pick without conversation.

"If you must know, we argued about 'bare ruined choirs where late the sweet birds sang,'" replied Aunt Fifi. "It's from a poem by Shakespeare, a sonnet about old age."

"That's what made his feet twitch?"

Aunt Fifi was silent for a moment, and all Becca heard was the quiet sound of berries dropping.

"Ow. I can't get my sleeve free," Aunt Fifi complained.

There was a long tearing sound. "Don't worry — it was just thorns coming out. The plumber thinks the sonnet is about baldness and losing your teeth. That 'yellow leaves, or none, or few do hang' refers to hair, or perhaps to old, discolored teeth, or teeth that have fallen out."

"You had a fight about rotten teeth?"

"Not rotten, discolored. It's an important issue," said Aunt Fifi. "There, I've finished this spot. I'm just going to move the ladder over."

The brambles rustled and snapped noisily as Aunt Fifi removed the ladder, then put it up in another place.

Becca reached into the bush again, and berries fell into her hands. With her boots she stamped down the stalks that threatened to snag her bare legs. She made a passage and burrowed into the middle of the blackberry vines. Under there it was cool and green. The berries had ripened among the dead branches of last year's growth, and thorns picked at her arms when she reached for them.

"This hurts!" she said. "And there's an old barbed wire fence poking into me, too."

"I told you it was a painful business," Aunt Fifi said cheerfully. "That's why I always come dressed to the nines. Oh, look at these! There are thousands of them up here, right where the sun hits them best!"

Becca heard her wrestle the ladder around and lean it up against the bushes.

"This is incredible," Aunt Fifi remarked. "I don't think anyone's picked here for years."

The ladder squeaked with each step and the brambles rustled noisily, as if they were talking among themselves.

Aunt Fifi's bucket clanged.

"Whoops!" she said. "Last step. Wow, these berries are as big as — "

The ladder creaked.

Aunt Fifi grunted strangely, sounding a bit like a hog.

Then Becca heard a great, slow crackling. It began as a rustle, became the sound of breaking branches, and then, drawing all the other crackling, snapping and pulling noises with it, became the loud, scraping, tearing sound of a million thorns letting go.

Aunt Fifi shrieked, and there was silence.

*　　*　　*

Becca backed out of her bramble burrow.

"Aunt Fifi? Are you okay?"

"Oh my."

Aunt Fifi's voice came from the middle of the bramble thicket, and as soon as she spoke there were more rustlings and cracklings, more prickly tearing noises.

"I can't move," she announced when the crackles had died down.

"Where are you?"

Becca waded through the dry grass at the edge of the bushes.

"I'm over here." Aunt Fifi sounded unusually quiet. "Keep walking. Ow."

Even talking seemed to make the brambles prickle and crack.

If it hadn't been for Aunt Fifi's hat, which had stayed on top of the brambles while the rest of her had crashed through, Becca might not have found her at all.

"I can see something blue," Becca called. "Is that your shirt?"

"Probably." Aunt Fifi's voice was very quiet.

"Are you going to crawl out?" Becca asked.

"No," said Aunt Fifi. "I can't move. And anyway because of the thorns I think I have to come out the way I went in, unless I want to turn into a bloody mess. I'm completely stuck here." She was so still that it was as though the bramble patch itself were speaking. "Don't worry, I'm not using bad language," she added suddenly.

"I can see the ladder," Becca said. It lay cock-eyed to the ground, tilted over where Aunt Fifi's falling weight had pulled it.

She started to climb along it, slowly and carefully, stopping with each step to wait for the brambles to settle under her.

There was Aunt Fifi's plaid shirt, her jeans, and finally her face, gazing up at Becca from the midst of the brambles.

"I can see you," Becca said.

"I didn't fall all the way to the ground," said Aunt Fifi. "I'm stuck in old brambles and stalks."

"I could get a log," Becca said. "I could roll it up from the beach and... "

But she knew it was impossible.

"'Consum'd with that which it was nourished by,'" Aunt Fifi said.

"What?" Becca wondered if Aunt Fifi's mind had started to wander. She'd heard about that sort of thing, that sometimes when terrible things happened to people, suddenly they started acting strange and saying odd things.

"It's a line in the poem the plumber and I argued about," Aunt Fifi said calmly. "Here I am, stuck in the very bushes that bore the berries that made such a good pie for me last summer. A pie, I have to add, that I was intending to share with the plumber until he showed himself to be such an oaf."

Becca thought Aunt Fifi was being silly, under the circumstances.

"Good thing you wore all those clothes," she said, trying to make Aunt Fifi feel better. "Think how scratched you'd be if you were dressed like me!"

"Dressed as I am," corrected Aunt Fifi.

"Well, anyway, there's a sort of skinny tree here that I could hold on to, to help pull you out. And there's a log I can stand on to pull you up. Then you could step back on to the ladder and crawl backwards, maybe, if it doesn't sink any more."

"If. Maybe." Aunt Fifi seemed to have become very philosophical. "My whole life is flashing before my eyes. But I'll try it. I have a feeling it's going to be excruciating. I didn't just fall into the blackberry bushes, you know. I'm right in the middle of the old barbed wire fence. Still, I can't stay here for the rest of my life and we can but try."

But when Aunt Fifi tried to sit up, the whole blackberry bush shuddered and crackled.

"I can't put my weight down," she told Becca. "It just makes me sink further."

Becca inched her way off the ladder and on to the log. It lay smothered in brambles, but still solid and steady under her feet. Out of the end of it grew a sapling — not thick enough for a person to climb but solid enough for Becca to hang on to while she gave Aunt Fifi a hoist.

"Can you reach me?" Becca asked. With one arm hugging the sapling, she stretched out the other until she could feel a hand under her fingertips.

"Got it!" Aunt Fifi cried. "Now I'm going to try to get up. Are you ready?"

Becca thought she was as ready as she could be. Either Aunt Fifi would pull her into the brambles, or Becca would pull Aunt Fifi out. It was as simple as that — as simple as falling off a log.

"Ready."

Becca tugged. Thorns tore. Stalks bent and crackled.

"Ow! Ouch!" cried Aunt Fifi. Slowly she came upright, even though she was still down there in the bushes.

"Well, that's some improvement," she said. "But my legs are stuck. They're stuck... "

Becca peered down.

"They're stuck in the barbed wire," Becca finished for her.

"The barbs have gone completely through my jeans," Aunt Fifi told her. "I can't even bend down to pull them out."

She tried to lift first one leg, then the other.

"It's no use," she said. "They're stuck in the brambles, too. There are thorns all through them."

Becca felt the whole expedition had become much too sweaty and uncomfortable, and they didn't even have their buckets full of berries. They had hardly started!

"Well, if you can't pull your legs out in your jeans, pull your legs out of your jeans. And I don't want to hear any more Shakespeare," she said.

"Pull my legs out of my jeans?" exclaimed Aunt Fifi. "But what about my boots? And Shakespeare didn't write about jeans, just about boots. 'Trouble deaf heaven with my bootless cries' — "

"We'll get your boots once you get up here," Becca interrupted her. "We can nab them with your blackberry stick."

"I can't believe I'm doing this," said Aunt Fifi.

She unzipped her jeans and gently lifted one leg out. She reached for Becca's hand. Becca thought her arm would pull right off her body as she hauled Aunt Fifi upwards. And then there was a horrible pause while Aunt Fifi hung at the end of Becca's arm, shook off the remaining boot and pulled her other leg up to join the first.

"Don't let go of me!" Aunt Fifi shrieked.

Becca hadn't the breath even to grunt.

Perched among the brambles on the log, Aunt Fifi was

silent as Becca fished for the boots with the hook on the blackberry-picking stick, and silent as she pushed her feet back into them.

"You look funny standing there in your shirt and underpants and boots," Becca said, before she leaned out to fish out Aunt Fifi's jeans.

"I feel mighty funny, believe me. And I still have to make it onto the ladder and down out of the bush. And we haven't even finished getting the berries."

"Can't we go home now?"

"Certainly not," said Aunt Fifi. "We need a lot more berries. We need enough for jelly, and for pie. Maybe I'll relent and invite that plumber over to join us after all."

* * *

They picked for another hour, naked legs and all. Aunt Fifi said it would take too long to pick all the thorns out of her jeans and she'd just deal with it later.

"I can't tell what's blood and what's blackberry juice," said Becca as they trudged home with the ladder and laden pails.

"You'll know when you go in the sea," Aunt Fifi predicted gloomily. "Your scratches will sting like the dickens. I just hope that plumber has come and gone, taking his clacking teeth with him."

"His teeth clack?"

"He has an old-fashioned pair of dentures that don't fit properly," Aunt Fifi said grumpily. "No wonder he has such peculiar ideas about Shakespeare."

Whether that made sense or not, Becca couldn't say. She thought life would be calmer and less painful once Aunt Fifi had gone back to the city with her blackberry jelly.

On the other hand, she was quite looking forward to dinner with the plumber.

5. Jelly

"Is THE plumber gone?" Aunt Fifi demanded as they clomped up the path to Gran's cabin, aching from the weight of the berries and criss-crossed with scratches.

"Why? Are you spoiling for another fight?" Gran inquired.

"Did his teeth clack?" Becca asked.

"Did his teeth clack?!" Gran repeated.

"Aunt Fifi says he has false teeth. She says they clack." Becca looked around. She thought it might be rather interesting if the plumber were still there. He'd probably never seen Aunt Fifi quite so decorated in scratches and missing her trousers, too.

"His teeth are perfectly reasonable," Gran said to Becca, but Becca didn't miss the dirty look she directed at Aunt Fifi. "Fiona, why do you tell this child such stories?"

"I was going to invite him to dinner," Aunt Fifi said, picking thorns out of her clothes.

"I'd like to stay on the plumber's good side," Gran said.

"I've had a sudden change of heart," Aunt Fifi told her. "My experience among the blackberries and barbed wire made me want to be a nicer person. Even though his teeth clack."

"His teeth do not clack, but go ahead and invite him. Maybe I'll invite Mac, too, since he's here for the weekend. And by the way, why aren't you wearing any trousers?"

* * *

"Ooh! Ow!" Becca screeched as they waded out of the sea the next morning.

Her legs and arms were laced with scratches that woke up when they were wet.

"Signs of an interesting life," said Gran. "I'm looking forward to one of your pies, Fifi. Although I can see that you both paid in blood."

"First we have to make jelly," said Aunt Fifi. "Becca is going to help."

"I am?" Becca had been planning a quiet day on the beach, letting her scratches get used to salt water. She thought that would take all day, and all her energy.

"You are," Aunt Fifi answered. "I hotted up the berries and dumped them in the bag last night, and now there will be lots of lovely juice!"

* * *

"That jelly bag looks familiar," Becca said after breakfast.

"It's one of your gran's pillow cases," said Aunt Fifi.

She squeezed the glistening, swollen bag, ran her hands down it so that wine-colored juice spread over her skin and trickled into the bowl below.

"It looks like blood," said Becca. "People would think you'd murdered someone in here if you spilled it."

"I won't," Aunt Fifi said. "Gran did once, though. A memorable occasion. For no reason anyone could discern, she had decided to hang the jelly bag in her van that year."

"Fifi! That's one of my good pillow cases!" Gran cried from the door of the shed. "I told you to pick out one of the old ones."

"I took what was closest to hand," Aunt Fifi said. "Look out, I'm coming through."

"I shouldn't even let you through!" Gran exclaimed. "I should lock you in here for the rest of the day. Imagine doing that to my good linen!"

For a moment Becca thought she might get her day on the beach after all, but Gran stood back and Aunt Fifi stalked past.

"You won't say that when you taste the jelly," she said calmly.

"I came to see if you wanted to go to the recycling depot with me, Becca," said Gran.

"I'd love — "

"She can't," said Aunt Fifi. "She's helping me."

Becca looked at Gran. Gran knew she loved the free store at the recycling depot.

"Never mind," Gran whispered. "She's only going to be here for a few days."

*   *   *

Aunt Fifi put the bowl on the table. The blackberry juice lay sluggishly, except when Becca bumped the table, and then it quivered and jiggled. It looked like something half alive, something that might creep out of the bowl, ooze across the floor and go on to live for years under Gran's cabinets.

"It doesn't look good," Becca said.

"It is ugly," Aunt Fifi agreed. "And there sure is a lot of it." She sounded pleased.

"First we wash the jelly jars," she told Becca. "That's a good job for you."

Becca couldn't believe that Aunt Fifi was going to make her spend the morning doing dishes. She could be at the recycling depot trying to find a pair of sequined shoes to match the boa she'd picked up last time she was there. She could be on the beach counting her scratches or digging for geoducks. She could be swimming, or visiting Kay next door who always had home baking around, or seeing how Mac's new house was coming along. Or scouting out kids on the beach who weren't either babies or teenagers.

Instead she was up to her elbows in dishwater.

"Is this what Mum means when she complains she never wanted to be a housewife?" she asked Aunt Fifi.

"I wouldn't know," said Aunt Fifi, clattering around with Gran's pots. "I can't believe your gran doesn't have a bigger jam-making pot. And all she has is this ramshackle hot-plate thing for when she doesn't want to light the wood stove!"

For Gran had a strange arrangement of four electrical elements set right into the top of her counter like a stove top. Underneath, instead of an oven, was the cupboard for pots and pans, muffin tins, mixing bowls and kitchen contraptions from the ancient past — things like potato ricers and meat grinders.

"I'm going to have to make about six batches to get through all this juice with this teeny little pot," Aunt Fifi went on. "It's all very well for her to abjure the domestic arts, but it isn't convenient for me."

"What's abjure?" Becca asked.

"Give up," answered Aunt Fifi. "'This rough magic I now abjure.' Shakespeare."

Becca sighed into the soapsuds.

* * *

"Now what?" she asked, when the last jelly jar had been set to boil.

"Put the lids in a pot to boil, too," Aunt Fifi said, measuring sugar. "One, two, three — I can never believe how much sugar this stuff takes. Four, five, six. Have you got those lids in?"

On one element the jars clinked and thumped with the pops of boiling water. On another the lids heaved and clattered. On the front element blackberry juice steamed sweet steam, filling the air with its heady aroma.

"This isn't so bad," Aunt Fifi said cheerfully, pouring

vast amounts of sugar into the juice. "There. Now you stir it. And stir it and stir it. Let me know when it starts to boil."

Becca hung her head over the pot and stirred, watching the dark juice seep into the white sugar. Aunt Fifi rustled around with newspaper, clean cloths and measuring cups.

"It's boiling," Becca reported. The juice foamed up and Becca stirred frantically. "It won't go down!"

"Keep stirring! Keep it going for two minutes. Here, I'll set the egg timer."

Becca stirred. The juice frothed and foamed, boiling up like glistening, crimson lava. Her hair stuck to her face and blackberry sweetness filled her nose, her lungs, her whole head.

"Ready," Aunt Fifi said. She turned off the element and began to pour hot juice into hot glasses. "Wipe off the rims. Use the tongs and put the tops on. Careful when you screw them down. They're hot."

Mum would never have asked Becca to do this. Aunt Fifi didn't have kids, so she didn't know what they weren't supposed to do. It was kind of fun.

"There, doesn't that look great?" Aunt Fifi asked, gazing at the eight perfect glasses of jelly. The morning sun beamed through them, making them shine with ruby brilliance.

"Taste!" She offered the jelly spoon.

"Yum! Can I go swimming now?" Becca asked.

"No," said Aunt Fifi. "We still have quite a few batches to go. If only Mum had a bigger pot!"

*　*　*

"Aren't you finished yet?" Gran asked, bursting into the house a long time later. "Sorry I'm so late. I met a couple of friends and we went to the café for lunch. When are you going to make pie? Want to go for a swim, Becca?"

"She's still helping me," Aunt Fifi said quickly. Her face was rosy and her hair was sticking out. Becca could see a smudge of jelly on the back of her neck where she'd scratched herself while holding the jelly spoon.

"And we haven't even had lunch," Becca said.

*　*　*

"If you've invited the man for dinner you must at least make something reasonable," Becca heard Gran instructing Aunt Fifi. "You can't serve blackberry jelly for dinner. And now I've gone and invited Mac, too! Maybe I should cancel."

"I'll make dinner, Mum!" Aunt Fifi said, filling the next batch of jars. "Look at that, will you? This makes twenty-eight. I'll start the pie in a while."

"How are you going to get them all home on the ferry without your car?" Gran asked.

"I'll manage. Becca? I need you again."

Washing her fifth batch of jars, Becca felt the day would never come to an end.

"We've run out of sugar," squawked Aunt Fifi, banging the cupboard door. "I thought there was another bag in here!"

"Can we stop?" Becca asked. The tide was coming in, the sky was blue, and her suit was hanging on the line, dry and ready to go.

"No. I still have all this juice to deal with," said Aunt Fifi. "Pop over to Kay's and see if she has some to spare. I'll start the pastry while you're gone."

Of course Kay had sugar. She had a huge bucket of it, and she gave it all to Becca.

"Use what you need," she said. "Here, have a cookie."

Becca lugged the heavy bucket back through the trees to Gran's.

*   *   *

"Things are getting tight," Aunt Fifi said, looking at the clock. "There's more than enough juice for one batch, but not enough for two. We'll just do it all together. Oh, this piddling little jam pot! Now, you wash up the last of the jars, and I'll get the juice heating. Then you can stir it while I roll out pastry for a pie."

More soapsuds. More jars, more lids, more boiling. Becca was boiling.

"Do I have to stir?" she asked. "It's so hot!"

"I had to fire up the wood stove to bake the pie," Aunt Fifi said, panting as she thumped with the rolling pin. The pastry was bumping up against the jelly jars on the kitchen table and clouds of flour puffed up, clouding the sparkling look of them.

"Mother has no counter space whatsoever," crabbed Aunt Fifi. The jars clinked and clanked against each other as she twitched the pastry around and began another bout of vigorous rolling. "How's that juice going?"

"It's getting there," Becca reported, but mainly she was looking out the window. Kay was down on the beach with her beach towel, and now she could see Mr. and Mrs. Keswick coming along with their towels and the floating thermometer they used in the sea.

"Marion's here, too," she told Aunt Fifi. Marion was Kay's sixteen-year-old granddaughter.

"It doesn't matter," said Aunt Fifi, thumping. "Stir. There."

She flipped the pastry into the pie dish.

"It's boiling."

Becca stirred slowly as Aunt Fifi measured sugar into the pot.

"Ten, eleven, twelve," counted Aunt Fifi. "I don't know — do you think that's enough? I'll throw in another just to be sure. Keep stirring now. Oh, how I hate this stove!"

Becca stirred. Aunt Fifi dumped berries into the pie shell.

"It's starting to boil," Becca said. "It's boiling high. It's way up."

"Just keep stirring!" Aunt Fifi commanded hastily, slapping a cover of pastry over the pie.

"I am." Becca gazed at the neighbors and Gran. They were wading into the bouncing sea, leaping into the waves of a northwest wind.

"Stir! Stir!" cried Aunt Fifi, brushing the crust with

milk and then stabbing it with a fork. She looked like she was trying to kill the pie.

"I am," Becca said. She saw Marion drop her towel and go racing into the waves, splashing and waving her arms.

Hot jelly spat at Becca's skin.

"Ow!" She looked down into the pot.

Juice was rising to meet her. Boiling, boiling. It boiled furiously. It frothed and foamed. It rose up seething toward the top of the pot.

"It's rising!" she cried.

"Stir!" Aunt Fifi commanded.

"I am! It's boiling! It's boiling hard!"

Clouds of steam rose into her face, breathed into her body.

"Stir! Stir!" cried Aunt Fifi, crashing the oven door open and banging it shut, poking the fire and clanging the poker.

"It's higher!" Becca shouted. "It's foaming up. It's climbing up! It's going to overflow!"

"Glory be!"

Aunt Fifi seized the wooden spoon and stirred madly.

"Turn the element off!" she shrieked, but Becca was transfixed. The sweet, dark juice was alive, moving and flowing, bubbling upwards, glistening, growing —

With a great sizzle the jelly boiled over, poured over the rim in a rich purple fountain, cascaded in ruby streams down the side of the pot, flowed under the element and dripped, congealing as it went, into the regions under the range.

"Oh, for heaven's sake!" exclaimed Aunt Fifi, unable for once to think of Shakespeare. "Oh, for crying in the sink!"

The jelly subsided. There was a dreadful smell of burned sugar.

Becca started to scoop what was left in the pot into jars.

"You'd better put the lids on," she told Aunt Fifi.

Aunt Fifi opened the cupboard under the range.

"I can't bear to look," she said.

"Put the lids on," Becca repeated, filling the jelly glasses while they were still hot. "Come on! It's the last batch."

Silently, Aunt Fifi cleaned the rims and capped the jars. Becca dumped the pot in the sink and washed her hands, all the way up to her elbows.

"It sure is sticky," she said. She couldn't imagine wanting to taste blackberry jelly again, ever.

"Sticky is not the word for it," said Aunt Fifi. "World-class adhesive, maybe."

"It's not as bad as slug guts," Becca assured her. "They are the stickiest glue in the history of the world. Once, when I was camping, I accidentally stepped on one with my bare feet. And its guts stuck to my foot for weeks, and when I felt it with my fingers, it felt like — "

"Thank you for sharing," said Aunt Fifi. "But I don't think — "

Gran poked her wet head through the door.

"Mum, you don't want to come in here," Aunt Fifi said. "You don't want to see this."

"All right, I won't," said Gran agreeably, and she went off to have a little douse in the outdoor shower.

Becca looked into the cupboard. Jelly had trickled down the sides of the pans and pots Gran stored there, had congealed thickly on the shelves. It had streamed down the inside of the cupboard door and pooled out on to the floor. It hung like richly colored icicles from the braces in the cupboard. On the cupboard doorframe, jelled drips hung, shining.

"Someone has to wash all this," Becca realized. "All the pots and pans, too. And the muffin tins."

"The mixing bowls and the potato ricer," said Aunt Fifi. "Who uses a potato ricer anymore?" she grumbled. "I'll do it. You go and swim. You've waited long enough."

Through the window, Becca could see her bathing suit on the clothesline. It was bobbing in the wind as though it could hardly wait to jump into the sea, but out on the beach, Kay and Marion were packing up their wet towels and the Keswicks had already headed up for their dinner.

"It's okay," she said, filling the sink for the twenty-seventh time that day. "I don't really feel like swimming. Anyway my scratches still hurt."

6. Runabout

~~~~~~

THE PLUMBER arrived by sea.

"And a good thing, too," remarked Gran, as Becca rowed them out to pick him up at the mooring buoy. "Pull on the starboard oar, Becca."

"I am."

Becca had to row hard. Waves were bouncing into the Zodiac.

"It will give Fifi time to collect her wits," Gran said. "She gets herself into these states. Hard on the port. And I do wish I hadn't invited Mac, too, if pie is all we have for dinner."

For after all, Aunt Fifi had not got beyond making a pie.

The plumber bobbed about in a fancy motorboat, trying to make fast to Inglenooks' mooring buoy.

"It's an addlepated place for a mooring buoy," Gran said. "This is no bay to spend the night in a boat. No protection and with the tide in and out so far there's no depth."

"He's just coming for dinner, isn't he?" Becca asked.

"With Fifi around we'll be lucky if he stays that long," Gran said. "Hullo, Merlin. Are you ready for a ferry ride?"

The plumber raised his red face, pushed back a shock of hair.

"I am," he said. "And look! A surprise! My brother-in-law told me to try out his boat, so I did some fishing on the way."

He brandished a salmon.

"You *are* a magician if you managed to snag one of those," Gran said. "Foresightful, too."

Merlin climbed over the stern of his boat and into the lifting, falling Zodiac. "Thanks for coming out to ferry me. I thought I might have to swim in."

* * *

"Look," said Gran. "It isn't hard, or even messy."

"What's this?" Becca asked, poking at the salmon's squishy bits.

"That's the liver. And look — here's its intestine and stomach. If we wanted, we could check out what it's been eating."

"No, thanks," said Becca. She stroked the salmon's beautiful silvery side.

Gran pulled the guts out and threw them into the sea. She sliced off the head and washed the fish.

"We'll leave the head for an eagle," she said.

Becca put the head on Mermaid's Rock.

"Is his name really Merlin?" Becca asked.

"It is. He's a wizard with pipes. At least, that's what his van says."

"Do you think they're arguing about Shakespeare?" Becca asked.

"They might be," said Gran. "We'll take the fish up and referee."

But Merlin and Aunt Fifi weren't arguing. Merlin was washing lettuce and Aunt Fifi was in the garden, snipping herbs.

"She's a busy woman," Merlin told Becca. He could hardly find room for the lettuce among the fifty-seven jars of jelly. "Did somebody die here?" he asked, looking at the stain on the floor.

*   *   *

"Dugald says it will blow," Becca reported, hanging up the phone. "Winds from the northwest, gusting to thirty knots."

"I may have to walk home," said Merlin, ripping up lettuce and watching his brother-in-law's boat rise and fall out by the mooring buoy. "Or perhaps you'd give me a lift, Isobel."

"Or I will," said Aunt Fifi. "Would you like a glass of wine? Or would you rather replace the washer in the kitchen tap first?"

"That would be lovely, thanks," Merlin said, taking the wine. "Fifi, dear, you don't even want to *think* about what I charge."

Gran glared at Aunt Fifi, but Becca thought her aunt was being unusually polite.

Merlin replaced the washer, and the salmon hissed quietly in the oven. Aunt Fifi packed the jars of jelly away and Becca set the table. Mac arrived and it turned out he, too, knew Merlin.

"When's that pump going to arrive?" he asked. "I need it in before I move on to the next stage of building. I have relatives coming and the sooner, the better. Here, Isobel — I brought you a nice bottle of my namesake to enjoy on chilly nights."

*   *   *

"So, Becca," said Merlin. "Is it my freckles that interest you or do I have something stuck in my teeth?"

Gran stared sternly at Becca, and Aunt Fifi smiled.

Becca didn't know what to say, so she looked at her plate. She couldn't tell the plumber that she was hoping to hear his teeth clack, or even to see them fall out.

"I was wondering…" she said.

Aunt Fifi smirked. Gran looked a warning at Becca, very serious. Even Frank watched her intently — but that was probably the fish.

"…how you got so interested in Shakespeare," she finished at last.

"Shakespeare?"

"More fish?" Gran asked. She thrust the remains of the salmon in Merlin's face. No doubt she was thinking of the time last summer when Becca had seen his feet twitching with argument.

But Merlin smiled. He had quite ordinary teeth, Becca thought, as she stared into his face.

"I used to be an actor," he said.

"A real actor?" Becca asked. "In theaters? I mean, on stage? A real Shakespeare actor?"

"Indeed."

"But how does a plumber get to be a Shakespeare actor?"

"You mean, how does an actor get to be a plumber," Merlin corrected her.

For a moment Aunt Fifi looked stunned, and even Gran was pink in the cheeks.

"An actor! So that's why you know nothing about the sonnets," said Aunt Fifi.

"Fiona!" Gran warned.

"What did you act in?" Becca asked.

"All sorts of things," Merlin replied. "Mainly the comedies. You know, plays with happy endings, all about love. I played almost every drippy young lover Shakespeare invented."

"Drippy!" gasped Aunt Fifi.

"Face it, Fifi," Merlin said. "All those young lovers are airheads. Just a bunch of pretty faces."

"Pretty faces!"

Becca looked at Merlin's beautifully freckled face with its rather ordinary teeth, and thought she could just see him as a handsome lover.

He grinned at her.

"I had a terrible accident," he related, as the wind beat against Gran's cabin. "I was acting this fellow who goes around sticking poems on trees."

"Orlando," said Aunt Fifi. *"As You Like It."*

Becca knew Aunt Fifi couldn't help naming the character and the play he came from. It was like Gran identifying birds.

"The same," Merlin said. "Well, we had these very lifelike trees, but of course they weren't exactly rooted to the floor. I went to nail up a poem and in a strange accident — whack! One of them fell and bashed me right in the face."

Aunt Fifi looked horrified. So did Gran. But Becca laughed.

"Well you may laugh," said the plumber. "That tree ended my career. It knocked out my front teeth, and a few others. That was the end of it. Whoever heard of a Shakespearean actor with no front teeth? No one. Even the oldest, most decrepit character in Shakespeare needs teeth. 'Last scene of all, which ends this strange eventful history,'" he said, suddenly sounding intense and even a little crazy, "'is second childishness and mere oblivion, sans eyes, sans teeth, sans taste, sans everything.'"

There was a little silence.

"'Sans' means 'without,'" he told Becca in his normal voice. "Without eyes, without teeth — you see? Shakespeare knew that when you lose your teeth, you've reached the end. Of your acting career, at any rate."

"But you have teeth," Becca pointed out.

"Completely artificial," Merlin said, tapping his front incisors. "Look!"

For the tiniest instant he removed them, and Becca saw a dark and toothless space. It made him look completely different, as though he did actually belong in a play, and wasn't Merlin at all. Then he put them back in and looked like the plumber again.

"That's... interesting," Becca said. No doubt this was the secret of the teeth-clacking.

"Remarkable," Aunt Fifi said.

"Yes," agreed Merlin. "You wouldn't think Shakespeare could affect your teeth so drastically. For a while there I thought I'd be eating through a straw for the rest of my days."

"I didn't mean your teeth," Aunt Fifi said, annoyed. "I meant, that you've acted in all those plays! You must know them through and through."

"I do," Merlin said. "I know them by heart."

He crossed his hands over his chest.

Aunt Fifi looked thoughtful as she cleared the dishes from the table. She was probably thinking about how she had called the plumber an oaf.

* * *

"This is terrific pie," Merlin said.

"Even on its own it would have made a superlative dinner," said Mac.

"One of your best, Fifi," Gran agreed.

"It must be all the blood," Becca said, showing Mac and Merlin her arms with their scabbed-over scratches.

"Yes," Merlin said. "No one tells you that acting Shakespeare or picking berries can be life-threatening. They just let you learn for yourself."

"Doing anything with Aunt Fifi can be life-threatening," Becca whispered. She liked the plumber and wanted to warn him.

"I believe you," he whispered back, but before Becca could tell him and Mac how Aunt Fifi had flooded the house with jelly today and fallen into the blackberry bushes yesterday, Aunt Fifi returned to the table.

"Let's take our coffee out to the deck," she suggested. "It's windy but nice. And we won't have to look at the dirty dishes."

"I'll do the dishes," Merlin offered.

"Later," said Aunt Fifi, and led the way out to the deck. She seized a mug of coffee and plonked herself in a deck chair.

"So you feel the young lovers are drippy," she said.

"Saps, to a man," Merlin agreed. "Lovely coffee."

"It could be that that's not the most important thing about them," said Aunt Fifi sternly.

"Of course it is! Think of Orlando's awful poetry!"

"Poetry!" cried Aunt Fifi. "What do you know about poetry?"

"Look at that boat," Becca said. "Isn't it kind of windy to be out in a boat?"

"It is," said Mac. "There'll be a gale force warning in

effect by tonight and gusts from the northwest up to fifty knots. That boat won't last a minute."

"What boat?" Aunt Fifi asked, but she hurried on. "Merlin, I don't know why you have this anger, this unreasonableness, about poetry! A man who used to act Shakespeare!"

"What's unreasonable about it?" Merlin demanded.

"Nobody would be silly enough to go out in a small boat in this weather," Gran assured Becca.

"Well, there's nobody in it," Becca reported. "It looks like it's all on its own."

"Another rescue!" predicted Mac. "What is it with you people and boats?"

Becca saw the light of the setting sun glint off the windshield. The boat hung on the crest of a wave, lurched and disappeared into the next trough.

"It's an inboard-outboard," Becca said. "Same kind Merlin came in."

"They aren't listening," said Gran. "In case you hadn't noticed. Woe is me! He's the only plumber on the island!"

Huge swooshing breakers tore and foamed into the bay and up on to the beach. On the point, great curtains of white spray tossed themselves carelessly straight up into the air, hung suspended for a moment and then fell back into the sea.

"Isn't that what you call broadside to the waves?" Becca asked.

"Broadside to the waves!" exclaimed Gran, leaping to

her feet. "It certainly is! Merlin, isn't that your brother-in-law's boat?"

"How can you say that, Fifi?" Merlin argued. "'Mind' and 'Rosalind' don't even rhyme, and that's one of Orlando's better efforts. What did you say, Isobel? What boat? Oh, great Pollux! Oh, Neptune's noggin!" Merlin cried, tearing down the steps to the beach. "Arnulf's boat! It's going to be wrecked!"

"Becca, it's time for a swim," Gran told her. "Run and get the suits — Fifi's, too. Hurry."

"I knew that mooring line was no good!" Merlin wailed. "I told Arnulf!"

"Mooring line, nothing," retorted Gran. "You need a few lessons in knots."

"I hope his plumbing skills are better than his boating skills," Mac remarked and jumped down on to the beach.

Panting, Becca pulled on her bathing suit. Gran and Aunt Fifi were out the door before her, running down the beach like a couple of fleeing goddesses Becca had seen once in a painting. They were like goddesses in sensible bathing suits. Even in the twilight she could see Aunt Fifi's long legs flash, and then Gran's. They raced past the wailing Merlin and ran out on to the sand and into the foaming breakers.

Becca caught up to them in the shallows.

"What are we going to do now?" she shouted. The wind blew her hair straight out from her scalp and hurled spray into her face.

"We have to catch the boat before the waves smash it on to the beach," Aunt Fifi yelled. "Come on!"

Becca seized Aunt Fifi's hand and headed into the oncoming seas.

"The water's warm!"

"It's lovely!" Gran and Aunt Fifi shouted.

*   *   *

Merlin's brother-in-law's launch had taken on a life of its own. It reared above them broadside to the cresting waves, and whenever Aunt Fifi jumped for the bow, it jerked out of reach.

"We want to turn it around," Gran hollered. "Take it in bow first."

Smooth white fiberglass rose high above Becca and dropped down before the next roller. Her hands slipped off the wet sides.

"Stand back, Becca!" Gran shouted. "It might hit you!"

In the dusk, in the bounding waves, the boat was like a huge clumsy animal leaping wilfully just out of reach.

It wallowed into a trough, and there was the low part of the stern where the motor was. It was made so people could climb over it. There were even handles to make it easier.

"Hey!" Becca called.

The wind blustered, the waves rolled, and nobody heard her.

The boat lifted, slid sideways.

Becca gripped the handle. A wave heaved the boat upwards and Becca went with it.

"Hey!" she shrieked.

"Becca!" Gran called.

"I've got it!" Becca yelled.

"Of course!" said Gran, suddenly hanging on to the transom next to Becca. "We can turn it from behind. Merlin! Fifi!" she boomed into the coming dark. "Mac!"

"Push," said Merlin, appearing beside Becca, dripping and warm. "Push, Fifi!"

Waves sloshed, lifted and pushed. Becca rose and fell so that sometimes her toes weren't even touching the sand. She and Merlin, Aunt Fifi, Mac and Gran shoved and pulled, tugging at the back of the boat. Seawater splashed into Becca's face, into her mouth. Little by little the stern went round; the bow pointed into the beach.

Aunt Fifi and the plumber each seized a gunwale and started to guide the boat into the shallows.

"Maybe we can take the motor off and haul the boat up onto the beach," Merlin hollered. "I could get Arnulf's boat trailer and tow it home. But it'll be too heavy to get up the beach with this big motor on."

"It won't work!" Aunt Fifi said. "You won't get the motor off a boat like this that easily. We should just haul it up and wait for morning and better weather." She sounded quite kind.

"You're right," Merlin said, pushing uselessly at the motor.

"Never mind," said Aunt Fifi. "It'll be safe on the beach."

"I don't dare leave it," Merlin replied. "It's not even mine! What if something happens to it?"

"We'll babysit it," Aunt Fifi told him.

"That's asking for trouble," Gran grumbled to Becca and Mac, as they pushed the boat forward until the waves beached it, gently enough, on the sand.

But Becca had suddenly realized something. First, that Aunt Fifi was having a great time, and second, that she liked the plumber.

*　*　*

Aunt Fifi took a thermos down to the boat, along with Gran's lantern and a couple of beach chairs. Merlin had already changed into dry things — a pair of Grandpa's old sweatpants with no elastic and a mustard-colored sweater full of holes. Gran kept them stored for such emergencies, but they left Merlin's wrists and ankles bare to the elements.

"Life is so eventful around you," Mac told Becca before he left. "What do you do to get these adults so wound up? Or is it just that your cousins aren't here for you to drag up and down cliffs, so you have to find some other excitement?"

"I didn't do anything!" Becca protested.

"So you say!" said Mac, and he departed, dripping, for his own cabin.

Becca looked down toward the beach. She could see

the tiny glow of Gran's lantern reflecting off the boat's shiny hull, making shadows of Merlin and Aunt Fifi.

"What do you think they're talking about?" she asked.

"They shouldn't be sitting out there together," Gran said gloomily. "And all night, too! No good will come of it. And he's the only plumber on the island!"

"And he promised to do the dishes," Becca said sadly, looking at the heaps of dirty plates.

7. Sailing

~~~~~~

IN THE morning the sea was calm. Merlin was gone, and so was his brother-in-law's boat.

"I don't know what Fifi took out in that thermos," Gran whispered to Becca, "but it did them no good."

"Did they argue?"

"What do you think?" Gran cried, throwing her hands in the air. "And he's the only plumber on the island!"

"Mother!" shouted Aunt Fifi. "Will you stop repeating yourself? You don't even have water to worry about!"

It was true. Gran's plumbing used rainwater that ran off the roof, through the downpipes and into her cisterns. In summers when there was no rain to replenish the cisterns, water had to be rationed. Everyone took turns carrying drinking water down from the community well and the plumbing was used only for non-drinking necessities — the toilet, washing dishes, and sometimes a very, very short shower. No baths! That was one of Becca's favorite things — the sea kept her clean when she visited Gran in the summer.

But not having a lot of water didn't mean, Gran said, that she wouldn't have plumbing needs. Or that she wanted to have to worry about finding a plumber who didn't have opinions about Shakespeare.

Aunt Fifi crashed about with crates of blackberry jelly. She said nothing, loudly.

Becca hugged her goodbye, even though she was so grouchy. Aunt Fifi relented and gave her a kiss.

"Aunt and niece by birth; sisters by blood," she said, pointing to her blackberry-picking wounds. "And soon you'll have another sister — or maybe a brother!"

She lugged her boxes of jelly on to the ferry. The scribble of scratches on her arms made her look like she had a rare skin ailment.

* * *

"What do we do now?" Becca asked Gran. The day suddenly felt empty.

"I always feel I need a rest after a visit from Fifi," Gran said. "Let's sit on the beach and have tea."

It was hard to believe that the wind had been fierce only yesterday. Becca leaned against the driftwood and stretched her legs out on the warm stone. The problem with sitting still was that she could now think about Mum, who was about to give birth, and Dad, who was going to help.

"I could be there," she told Gran.

"You could be," Gran agreed. She seemed to know at once what Becca was thinking. "But I'm glad you decided to come be with me instead. And the baby might not be born for a week, or even two. And I would be lonely without you."

"Really?"

"Yes. Is that so amazing?"

"Even when I use *poutine* in Scrabble?"

"Let's not go too far," said Gran.

"She'll be little," Becca said, thinking of babies again. "Tiny."

"That she will," answered Gran. "Or he. You'll have to look out for her. Or him."

"And she'll come here when she's only a day old, or maybe two," said Becca.

"We'll have a birthday party," said Gran. "The whole family will arrive and we'll welcome him or her with splendid splendor — a party! You won't be an only child anymore."

"Let's go tide-pooling," Becca said. Suddenly she wanted to be up and doing, not sitting on the beach thinking about parents and babies and only children.

So they went around to Midshipman Bay and looked under a few stones, and in among the sea lettuce and in the drippy regions underneath rocky overhangs.

Becca found sea cucumbers and sea anemones. She found starfish prickly and purple, skinny and red, and slimy and brown. She saw one that squirmed and one that had seventeen legs. She found a moon snail and a sea-collar made of moon-snail eggs. She saw a cluster of fish eggs clinging under a rock.

But no matter what Becca found, Gran talked about families. She talked about scientific classification, and families and sub-families. She talked about the different ways sea animals have babies. When they looked at the moon snail she told Becca that every moon snail is male and female, both at once, and when they looked at the fish eggs she told her about how midshipman dads hang around and protect the eggs after the mum fish has swum off and forgotten all about them.

"Families can be strange," Becca said, carefully not thinking of Lucy and Alicia and their mum Aunt Catriona, or of her older cousins Mollie and Ardeth and their parents Auntie Clare and Uncle Clarence; studiously not thinking of Aunt Fifi, or even of Auntie Meg and Uncle Martin, who would arrive tonight. Especially not thinking of Dad and Mum and her soon-to-be sister or maybe brother. Because the whole point of going tide-pooling was not to think about these things.

"Can I phone Mum and Dad when we get back?" she asked, giving up at last. "Just to see what's happening?"

Then, hoping that Gran would stop talking about babies and families, Becca took her to look at sea urchins.

"But the seaweed there is so slippery," Gran said. "And the tide's up far enough now that we won't be able to see them very well."

"We'll be able to see them," Becca said, pulling her along by the arm. "Look! The color is just the same as Aunt Fifi's jelly."

"I'm surprised you're willing to think about that," said Gran. "But it is, rather."

In the sunshine and through the sloshing waves of incoming tide, the sea urchins waved crimson spines and glittered.

"Look!" Gran exclaimed. "Look at all the little ones!"

She leaned out over the edge of the sandstone and peered down into the drop-off, all along the side of the rock where tiny urchins clung.

"Isn't that lovely!" said Gran. "It's — whoops!"

And with a huge splash she fell into the sea, dragging Becca with her.

She didn't mention babies once as they swam home in their clothes.

* * *

"Well, now I've almost recovered from Fifi," Gran said as they dripped up the beach. "Who's coming tonight? I can't keep track."

"Auntie Meg and Uncle Martin," Becca said. "And I want to go sailing. I'm going to get Uncle Martin to help me take out *Glaucous Gull*."

"Good luck," said Gran. "We've had a lot of adventures in that boat and I'm not sure you want to repeat most of them."

* * *

"We could rig *Glaucous Gull*," Uncle Martin agreed the next morning, inspecting Gran's boat.

"The rigging has fallen apart, but we have all the bits," Gran said. "I'm just not sure the boat's entirely sound."

"It's a unique design for a sailing vessel," Uncle Martin said, and Becca didn't think it was a compliment.

"Well, a friend of Grandpa's invented it," said Gran. "It's one of a kind."

"You can say that again," said Uncle Martin.

"It will be okay," Becca said. "Help!" She tugged at the upside-down boat.

They pulled it out of the bushes and turned it right side up.

"*Glaucous Gull*, eh?" Uncle Martin said. "Sounds like something you'd do into a handkerchief. Let's see, first we'll mend this hole, dear me, and then, hmm..."

He inspected gunwales and oarlocks, transom and tiller.

"It's all green," Becca said. "Seaweed's growing on it."

"It's algae from sitting under pines and weather," said Uncle Martin. "We'll scrub it away."

The sun shone, the breeze blew, and all morning Becca and Uncle Martin mended and cleaned, scraped, scrubbed and untangled wires.

"We're just about done!" cried Becca, hoisting the sail in jerks.

"Beeswax," advised Uncle Martin. The next time Becca hauled on the line the sail flew up the mast, flapping and snapping.

"There you go!" cried Uncle Martin. "She's set!"

* * *

Auntie Meg didn't want to go sailing.

"Oh, please," Becca begged.

"I'll be seasick," Auntie Meg said. "I'm feeling queasy already. And I don't know anything about sailing."

"I'll sail," Becca offered.

"You're a bit small," Uncle Martin said. "You can be my ship's boy — girl, I mean."

"You be careful," Gran advised them. "Dugald says it's going to blow later and you don't want to be caught in it."

"We'll just take her out for a spin," said Uncle Martin. "Will you come, Meg? First mate?"

"I guess so," Auntie Meg agreed, "if it's only for a little spin."

"Cross my heart," said Uncle Martin, and he gave her a big fat kiss.

Becca had to look away.

Auntie Meg had married Uncle Martin last summer, and now they lived together on a little island like Gran's. But Uncle Martin was often away at sea, tugging and barging south, north, back and forth. Perhaps that was why they were always so mushy. In any case, Becca wasn't sure she wanted to be cramped into *Glaucous Gull* with them if they were going to carry on like that.

"All set then?" asked Uncle Martin.

They carried *Gull* into the sea.

Gran stepped back. They were off.

* * *

Becca sat forward of the mast. She fit there, wedged by her life jacket. She could twist and look forward and say when there were rocks sticking up, or she could look back and see Auntie Meg amidships and Uncle Martin in the stern.

Auntie Meg rowed them out of the shallows.

"We'll tack across the bay and see how she goes," said Uncle Martin. "Ship the oars!"

Auntie Meg drew in the oars. The sail shook itself loudly and swelled tight.

"Here we go!" Auntie Meg smiled and Uncle Martin leaned over to kiss her, so that the sail spoke sternly and *Gull* tried to dip into the sea.

"Oops!"

Uncle Martin grinned and they were underway. *Gull* plowed the water. Becca's hair blew and she looked ahead — first into burbling foam at the bow and then at the blue field of sea before them.

And that was all right. Auntie Meg thought so, too, and when Uncle Martin said, "How about taking her out into the strait?" Auntie Meg laughed and said, "Oh, Martin, I wouldn't pin your wings for anything!"

Uncle Martin brought the *Gull* about and set them flying into the broad strait, looking for all the world like he was going to kiss Auntie Meg again. But Becca turned to watch the water curl out around them and felt the wind blow into her as if she, too, were a sail or a seabird.

She felt like she could fly.

"Look at the white horses!" called Uncle Martin.

"What do you mean?" Becca shouted.

"Look at the swell! The waves!"

Becca saw blue dark seas hurry toward her, gathering until they spilled into crests, foam flying. They swelled and heaved under *Gull*, let her down with a lurch and carried their bubbling white manes on with them.

Slap! A white horse climbed into the boat and doused Becca.

"Ow!"

"Sorry!" said Uncle Martin. "We'll head south and ride with them!"

He brought them about and white horses stopped trying to climb in. Becca hung over the bow as *Gull* galloped, carried by rushing seas. Hair blew into her mouth. Water boiled at the bow.

"Can I sail?" she asked.

"No," Uncle Martin said. "You be the lookout."

Becca looked out. What was there to look out for? Mounds of water rising beneath her, then passing on ahead.

She licked salt from her skin. She wasn't too young, she thought. She was strong enough to sail.

"I think we should turn back now," said Auntie Meg.

"Just a little longer," begged Becca. She loved this fast galloping ride.

"Well, let me have a go," Auntie Meg said, so Uncle Martin handed over the tiller and they traded seats.

Why does she get a turn and not me? Becca wondered.

Auntie Meg didn't know anything about sailing. She had said so herself.

She watched as Uncle Martin gave Auntie Meg directions about how to come about, to jibe, to spill the wind. Auntie Meg sailed them past Anderson Point, past Bouldings' and on toward Mayfield Point. The sea carried them, and the wind. *Gull* flew. Becca and Auntie Meg sang.

"Betsy had a baby and she dressed it all in white," they sang. "Heave away, Johnny, all bound to go…"

Uncle Martin didn't sing. He had become thoughtful, with his forehead wrinkled up and his eyes kind of serious-looking, as though he was concentrating on something very, very important.

"Ready about!" called Auntie Meg.

The boom slammed across and *Gull* leaned the other way. Becca was glad she was stuck where she was, padded with a life jacket.

Something was wrong with Uncle Martin. He looked as though he was thinking so far inside himself that he couldn't see *Gull*, or Becca, or Auntie Meg, or even the sea around them.

Something was wrong with Uncle Martin, and something was wrong with the way the sailing was going.

"We're going backwards," Becca said.

"What?" Auntie Meg stopped singing.

"We used to be across from that tree, and now we're behind it."

"I see."

Suddenly Uncle Martin hung over the gunwale and made a dreadful sound.

"Oh, poor Martin," said Auntie Meg. "Well, don't worry. I'll skipper for you."

Uncle Martin made another awful noise. It made Becca think of sea cucumbers, because Gran had told her that when they get scared, they spew. But sea cucumbers wouldn't make a noise like a very bad drain, the way Uncle Martin was.

Auntie Meg brought *Gull* about again. "Maybe if we head out, we'll get a stronger run against the current," she said. Becca had never seen her look so serious.

"We're still going backwards," Becca reported later. "I can't see Bouldings' anymore."

"She may be a gull but she sails like a penguin," said Auntie Meg shortly. "And the current is against us now and so is the wind. I don't know how we're going to get home."

"Maybe we could use the oars, too," Becca said loudly over the sound of the wind and Uncle Martin's noises. "Sail and row!"

"How can I do that?" asked Auntie Meg, bothered. "I can't sail and row! It's not sensible."

"I — can — sail!"

Becca's words came in jerks. White horses tried to climb into *Gull*. *Gull* jumped and banged the bottom of a sea hill.

"What?"

"I can do it!" Becca cried.

"We have no choice," Auntie Meg agreed at last.

Becca crawled aft, and Uncle Martin drooped up to the bow. He hardly fit there, but half of him was hanging out of the boat anyway. Becca saw his face as they passed. He looked gray and a bit corpse-like — not at all his usual adventurous seaman self.

"Take this line," ordered Auntie Meg. "It's the main sheet. It lets the boom and sail in and out."

"I know! I was listening! And this is the tiller," Becca said, grasping it. "It goes back and forth like this. Just like the Zodiac." She waggled it.

Auntie Meg looked astonished.

"Okay, so you do know," she said. "I'll row now, and you do your best with the sail, and together we'll get this *Gull* back to her nest."

"Double power," Becca said.

"Right."

The tiller thrummed under Becca's hand, and the main sheet cut into her fingers. *Glaucous Gull* headed up the strait, Becca at the helm. Auntie Meg got to work with the oars.

"Keep the sail tight!" she directed Becca. "Look at the sail! Feel the wind!"

She didn't have to tell her. Becca put her face to the wind, pulled hard and silenced the raging sail.

Auntie Meg heaved on the oars.

Uncle Martin kept to himself, way up in the bow.

Gull labored up one sea, and then another. The wilful sail pulled at Becca and she had to hang on with both hands. The tiller twitched under her arm. She let the sheet out and felt the tiller's lively tremble. Sailing made sense to her.

"We're not going backwards any more."

Bouldings' cabin was back in sight.

"We've a long way to go," Auntie Meg said grimly. Sweat glistened on her.

But Becca could see they were gaining. The current flowed and Auntie Meg pushed back. The wind blew and Becca leashed it. The breeze answered to her. *Gull* was gaining.

"How is it you're such a good sailor?" Auntie Meg wondered. "Afraid to swim with your face in the water, but no problem out here in a small-craft warning?"

"It isn't a small-craft warning," Becca said. "Dugald said gusting fifteen to twenty knots. He never calls that a small-craft warning."

The seas crashed and chattered, and sometimes the sail spoke, drowning out the horrible sounds of Uncle Martin. Becca commanded the ship, and Auntie Meg was the extra motor.

Gull climbed the watery ranges.

*   *   *

A long time later, Becca sang out, "Centerboard up!"

She had flown *Gull* into Gran's bay.

"Oh, Martin!" Becca heard Auntie Meg say, but she didn't look. Instead she kept her eyes on her course, her hand on the tiller, and skippered *Gull* gently up to the sandstone.

8. Seafire

A UNTIE M EG and Uncle Martin stayed for three days, and Becca learned more about sailing. The winds were lighter and Uncle Martin had no more trouble with seasickness.

"It happens once in a while," he said. "I had a headache and I was over-tired from coming off a night watch. But there you go. I thought you were too young to sail and you proved me wrong, so it had its good side. We need to get you a decent boat."

"Maybe I can take Mollie and Ardeth sailing," Becca said as she hugged him and Auntie Meg goodbye. "They're coming tomorrow."

Becca loved Mollie and Ardeth. They built the best sandcastles in the world, and last year they'd made a raft and the three of them had paddled all the way to Anderson Point. They'd played Sardines, Capture the Flag and Kick the Can. They'd taken Becca for hikes and picnics with their friends from around the bay — Kathy and Frances and Tasha. Mollie and Ardeth loved doing things, but unlike Aunt Fifi, their adventures didn't always involve pain, and unlike Lucy and Alicia, they didn't usually involve getting into trouble.

But Becca could see from the instant Mollie and Ardeth arrived that this summer was different.

They were big. They always had been, but this summer they loomed and towered. They bounded about with great, strong bodies, laughing at things that didn't make sense to her. They were fifteen, and twins.

"Let's swim!" they cried, hurling clothes as they dug for their bathing suits.

They ran into the water with Becca between them, swinging her over the waves.

* * *

But the next morning they slept late.

"Let's swim," Becca said, poking the lumps in sleeping bags. "Let's go sailing."

"They're still asleep," said Gran — quite unnecessarily, Becca thought. "But there's nothing to stop you and me from going swimming."

Becca could hardly wait for them to wake up.

She and Gran swam, made and ate breakfast, did the dishes and pumped a supply of drinking water from the well. They had coffee with Kay, visited the Free Store and shopped at the farmers' market.

But when they got home, Mollie and Ardeth were still asleep.

"It must have been a long trip," Becca said.

Gran smiled.

"Probably," she said. "Let's pick the last of the lavender."

"And the one tomato?" Becca asked, for Gran's garden looked rather sad in spite of all the spring-time labor. "What happened to the peas?"

"Robins got them," Gran said. "Slugs, too. Here's a basket for lavender."

Becca loved the deep, oily scent of lavender. She picked each stem carefully, thinking of last summer.

"Last year when it was windy we played in the waves before breakfast," she said. "It was the very first day after they got here. Remember?"

"I remember," said Gran.

"Why are they so sleepy?"

"Sleep is like food for them," Gran said. "You'll probably be like that too in a few years."

"Never," said Becca.

They took a long time up in the garden, and when they returned to the cabin, Mollie and Ardeth were reading.

"What are we going to do?" Becca cried, jumping on to Mollie's lap. "Let's sail! I know how to sail now!"

Mollie laughed and gave her a squeeze.

"No, let's read! Right now we're going to read, and then later we'll go for a swim."

*   *   *

Every day it was the same. Mollie and Ardeth slept, and then they read. Then they napped. They would play for a very little while — go for a swim or take out the Zodiac, but only row it as far as Anderson Point, and then they would insist on coming back to Gran's almost at once, and when they were there they would read again for a long, long time. Becca liked books, too, but she wanted to *do* something. And Gran wouldn't let her sail alone.

"They're only here for four days!" Becca wailed. "And two of them are already over! When are we going to start having fun?"

"You've been having fun!" Gran protested. "Yesterday you swam with them, and the day before they took you out in the boat!"

But it wasn't enough — a few bursts of fun in between stretches of reading or sleeping. They even napped in the afternoon. Like babies!

"There's something wrong with them," Becca insisted. "It's not fair!"

"Becca, out!" Gran said suddenly. "I will not listen to you moan for another minute. Go pick some rosemary. And don't forget to close the gate!"

As if she would! This visit was even worse than having no one around. Becca wished it was over.

That night when she went to bed, she peered over the edge of the loft, down at the heads of Mollie, Ardeth and Gran, all bent over their books. Evening was the time to read, Becca thought. Or rainy days. She could understand that. But summer days — they were the time to explore, to swim, to play hard and to have fun.

Mollie and Ardeth had no life at all.

* * *

Long after she'd fallen asleep, Becca awoke. Something smelled delicious, and even though it was far into the night, there was a light on below. She squirmed to the edge of the loft.

What had wakened her? Was it the smell? Popcorn and butter and something else — something so sweet and enticing that it had almost seemed to shake her awake.

Or was it Mollie?

Mollie was squawking. She was laughing so hard she was leaning over sideways, her face buried in her arms. She made little squeaking snorts and pounded her fist helplessly on the table.

She and Ardeth were playing Scrabble.

"Hand over the popcorn," Ardeth whispered. "Don't be such an animal. You sound like a pig."

"What are you doing?" Becca asked. "Can I have some?"

"Becca!"

Ardeth smiled and got up. She stood under Becca and held out her arms.

"Come on down!" she said quietly. "It's a midnight feast!"

Becca slipped down the ladder.

"Help yourself!" Ardeth whispered. "Mollie, if you don't stop laughing you'll have to go outside! You'll wake up Gran."

"There, I won," Mollie announced, stuffing her mouth with popcorn.

It wasn't just popcorn, it was caramel popcorn. It was like eating clouds. Becca's mouth seemed to rain when she tasted it.

"Are you still playing Scrabble?" she asked. "Can I play?"

"We're finished," Mollie said. "But now we're going to — "

She stopped and looked at Ardeth.

"We're going swimming," she whispered. "Do you want to come?"

"What about Gran?"

"Sh! She doesn't know," Ardeth said.

"It's our secret, heh-heh!" Mollie boasted, and she gave a great wink.

It was terribly dark when they tiptoed on to the beach, but after a moment Becca's eyes changed, or the stars grew brighter, or perhaps the water began to glow. Something changed and Becca could see, faintly, the stones at her feet.

"Come on," Ardeth said. Although Gran couldn't possibly hear them, Ardeth spoke quietly. It seemed as if the bay itself might be asleep, silently rocking reflections of the stars.

As they crunched over snails and dried seaweed, Becca thought she heard other movements, footsteps not their own.

"Stop," she said, tugging at Mollie's hand. "What's that?"

"It's only Marion," Ardeth said.

"Is Marion coming, too?"

Marion joined them and panted, "I almost fell over Dad and Mum! They were sleeping on the porch and I didn't even know!"

Mollie stifled her laughter, but mysteriously Becca seemed to hear it anyway — a chuckle from somewhere along the beach. Out from the trees stepped Tasha, almost as if she'd been waiting.

And down on the sand was Ardeth's friend Frances, and Sarah who worked at the store.

"Let's leave our clothes here," Mollie said. "Where it's dry. We'll go down to the water while we wait for the others."

"What others?"

"A festival of friends," Ardeth murmured.

The stars changed as they waited. For one thing, there were more of them, a great swoop of sparkling, magical dust. The Big Dipper, the only constellation Becca knew, was lost in the multitude that shone there.

For another, some of the stars darted about. Becca saw them zip, dazzle and disappear. Twice, yellow fire fell out of the sky, leaving a trail of sparks that glowed, then faded almost instantly.

"What are they doing?" she asked, but nobody heard her, or even seemed to notice the stars.

Instead Ardeth said, "Here come Kathy and Sue. It's time to go."

One by one, they let their towels drop to the beach.

Holding the hands of Mollie and Ardeth, Becca waded into the black water in a company of girls.

There was no turning back, even when the night water shrank her skin. The shapes of Kathy and Sue, Frances, Marion and the others gleamed like a pale grove about her. The only sound was of water disturbed by arms and legs, water that carried broken reflections of stars.

"Do they fall into the water?" Becca asked, for in the darkness she could see the sparkle of a thousand stars where she walked. It was as if the reflections had sunk, or the stars that had fallen before had somehow started a new life underwater.

"Do what fall in the water?" Ardeth asked.

"The stars. There are stars all over my legs."

Becca stopped walking.

"Well, you can't see them now," she said, confused. "Where did they go?"

She walked and lights prickled in the sea. A sweep of glitter billowed in her wake.

"Wow!" Ardeth exclaimed quietly. "Look, you guys, there's tons of it!"

"Tons of what?"

"Phosphorescence!" Ardeth said. "Luminescence!"

"What?"

"Little plants and things that light up," Ardeth said.

"Seafire," Mollie muttered. "Sealight! That's what some people call it. It's a natural wonder."

One by one, the gleaming girls sank into the sea, and

Becca did, too, staying close to Ardeth. Sarah and Frances squeaked at the cold as they went. The others just sighed and started to swim.

"I've never seen so much," Ardeth whispered.

It was as though they were clothed in light. When Becca lifted her arm, glitter dripped from it. She saw stars in Ardeth's wet hair and even on her teeth. The girls around her twinkled and waved glowing arms like angels' wings.

"Heavenly bodies!" Mollie said. "We're like stars!"

A school of fish flashed away like fireworks, leaving trails of light that winked and faded, just like the ones Becca could see even now up in the Milky Way.

"Is this falling stars, too?" she asked. "Do falling stars happen in the sea?"

"Holy cow!" Ardeth said. "No, it's — look up, you guys, look up!"

And each one of the starry girls lifted her face and saw what Becca was already seeing — a shower of meteors flashing in the August night.

*   *   *

Becca slept in the next morning, but still, she woke up before Mollie and Ardeth.

"Goodness me," Gran grumbled. "I don't know where all these dirty cocoa cups came from. Someone used my whole collection of mugs! And all these wet towels, and there's not a bathing suit to be seen! How did that happen, I wonder?"

But Becca could tell Gran was smiling, really.

That was when the phone rang.

"Becca!" said Dad. "Darling Becca. Your sister is here!"

9. Mothers and Pups

A SISTER! thought Becca. What would that be like? Mollie and Ardeth had each other, but they were twins, which was special somehow. Alicia and Lucy were different ages, but they were still close enough to have adventures together. It was like they were friends, even if they argued sometimes. But Becca thought a baby sister, one who was newborn, wouldn't be quite like that. Not quite a friend — more like a pet.

And even though Mollie and Ardeth did their very best to describe sisterhood to her, Becca felt she had no idea.

"Sometimes it's grotty and sometimes it's great," Mollie said.

"I don't know," Ardeth said. "I'm so used to having a sister I can't really say. I wish Mollie wouldn't wreck my clothes all the time though."

"I don't wreck your clothes!" protested Mollie. "Those shorts were already torn. And it's not my fault Frances spilled cocoa all over them!"

"Oh, sure," Ardeth replied. "Anyway, I'm sorry we

have to go back to work, Becca. It'd be so much better to be here to meet our new cousin than trying to stop a bunch of eight-year-olds from drowning each other at Paradise Ridge Camp."

"Or, as we like to call it," Mollie said, "the Heights of He —"

"I'm sorry we've been such slugs," Ardeth said quickly. She gave Becca a big hug. "But that was a superb night swim."

She and Mollie went off to meet Kay, who was giving them a lift on the early ferry. Becca and Gran were left standing on the deck in their bathing suits, ready for a morning swim.

"People are always leaving," Becca said.

"And coming," Gran reminded her.

She took Becca into the sea.

"Practice the crawl," Gran suggested. "You need to spend more time with your face in the water."

Waves reached for Becca.

"When will they get here?" she asked. The sea pulled at the sand underfoot.

"Not until dinnertime," Gran said.

Today Mum and Dad were coming. And her new sister. She could hardly wait.

"Come on!" Gran marched into the water.

"It's kind of wavy!" Becca said. The waves pushed at her legs. Sea froth nudged her.

"It's not bad," Gran said, bobbing nearby. "It's better when you're deeper."

What Gran said was true. Becca paddled through breaking waves, head high, until she too bobbed up and down.

"You don't put *your* face in," Becca said.

Gran laughed.

"Watch out or the sea will do it for you," she said.

And at that moment, a rough-and-tumble wave poured over Becca and went on its way chuckling.

"It tickles," Becca complained.

"Look out!" cried Gran, but before Becca could look the next wave rumbled her, and the next.

Inside the wave it was green, and bubbles were sparks in the sun. For the next wave, Becca took a great breath and pushed her face into the tickliest part, just where water curled to meet her. Then she turned and rocketed toward the shore, pushed by the sea.

She didn't hear Gran until she was back standing on the sandstone.

"What's that following you?" asked Gran, her voice high with surprise.

A silver creature paddled there, right at Becca's feet. It swam toward Becca and she jumped. It turned and swam into the shallows. It heaved about with the sea's wash, almost lost in the colors of barnacles, rockweed, water and stone.

"It's a seal! It's a baby — "

The seal pup lifted its face. It gazed at Becca with dark, dark eyes, whiskers sparkling.

"Oh, it is so cute," she breathed.

"Don't touch it!" Gran warned her.

Becca knew. If you touch a seal baby, its mother won't take it back. Last summer tourists who hadn't known about seal mothers had fed a baby seal and touched it, and its mother had abandoned it. Someone had had to come and take it away.

Becca stepped back.

The baby seal was tired. The waves kept on washing, washing, and it couldn't rest. At last it pulled itself right out of the water. It lay on the beach and looked at Becca.

"You see what happens when you swim underwater," said Gran seriously. "The seals think you're one of them."

Becca looked at the baby seal, and at the other people and their dogs wandering about far down the beach.

"I'll have to babysit," she said.

"What?" Gran asked.

"What if people don't know and they try to touch it? Then its mum won't take it back. I'll have to babysit it."

She sat on a lump of stone. The seal pup flopped toward her and she pulled up her feet.

"Will you bring me my breakfast?" she asked.

Gran brought her granola and blueberries and the seal went to sleep.

* * *

"Mum wouldn't let me sit out here without my hat," Becca said to Gran when she came back to collect the breakfast things.

"You need more than a hat," Gran said.

She came back with Becca's hat and an umbrella with a broken spoke.

"What about you?" Becca asked from under the shade. She twirled the umbrella like a parasol.

"I can't stay," Gran said. "I have a lot of work today, getting ready for our next visitors and cleaning up after our last ones. Will you be all right?"

"Of course!"

Becca watched. The sun rose in its arc, the tide ebbed, and the seal slept. Becca studied its silver skin, stippled with marks like shadow. She saw the creamy fur of its tummy — almost yellow — and its tail hanging over the back flippers. It looked like a dog.

But it woke up and mewed like a cat, and looked up at Becca.

Becca wasn't sure what to do. She didn't speak seal language, but she thought she understood well enough. It missed its mum.

"Your mum's just out fishing," she assured it. "She'll be back!"

The seal mewed again.

"Don't cry," Becca begged.

The seal pushed itself up on its flippers and slid toward her.

"Don't come too close," she warned, and drew her feet up. "Maybe you should have a little swim."

The wind had died down, and the waves. Even under her parasol Becca was hot.

"It's not really safe here!" she said fiercely. "You should tell your mum to leave you where there aren't so many people."

People were coming along the beach with a pair of dogs, and she didn't know what to say.

"Oh, look! A baby seal!"

"Don't touch it!" Becca said. "You're not supposed to touch it."

"Wow! Look at it, Mum!"

The children rushed in and the seal inched toward them.

"Don't let it touch you," Becca said. "Its mum will abandon it if you do."

She jumped off the rock. She didn't know what to do about this friendly little seal. It seemed to think everyone was its mother.

"We won't. We know about that." The woman put the dogs on the leash. "Come away, kids."

"But it's so cute!"

"They say you should phone Fisheries if it's left longer than twenty-four hours," the woman told Becca.

Twenty-four hours! That was a whole day, and over-night, too. Becca looked up at the cabin desperately, but Gran was nowhere in sight.

"Come on, kids."

The three of them pranced up the beach at last. Becca watched enviously. They were free to go and she was stuck here, in charge, somehow, of this baby.

The seal turned its huge, mysterious eyes up and gazed at her helplessly.

*   *   *

"How are you doing?" Gran asked. "What would you like me to bring you for lunch?"

"Only lunch?" Becca asked. It felt like suppertime. So far she had defended the seal baby against eight humans and three dogs. "When will its mother come back?"

"I don't know! You don't have to guard it, you know," Gran said. "You could let it take its chances, like most things in nature."

Becca considered. The seal mewed again and closed its eyes.

"No. I'll stay. When will Mum and Dad get here?"

"Not until later. You've got lots of time."

But Becca didn't want time. She wanted Mum to come now — the seal's mother and her own.

"I read a story once," Becca said. "About a seal who swam into shore and took off her skin and turned into a woman. But then she couldn't turn back into a seal because some man stole her skin. She was called a selkie." She looked at the seal. "Maybe this is the opposite."

"What do you mean?" asked Gran.

"I mean, maybe this is a girl who can become a seal, but someone took her girl-skin so she has to stay a seal. And now she's here on this beach, hoping her family will recognize her."

*   *   *

"Let's see," said Becca, talking to the seal since there was no one else to talk to after Gran had gone back up to the cabin. "Gran says that seals are called pinnipeds because they have fin feet."

The seal gazed up at her and slapped one of its fin feet on the stone.

"I'll call you Pinny," Becca said. "Too bad you can't find your girl-skin. If you did, we could go for a swim together. We could swim across the bay and prove what strong swimmers we are. Or we could go at night! Or maybe, if there was a bit more wind, we could take out *Glaucous Gull* and sail to Camas Island all on our own. What do you think?"

The seal lifted itself up on its front flippers. Its wide, dark eyes seemed to be trying to tell Becca something, but she couldn't tell what.

"It's all right, Pinny," Becca said. "Our mums will come soon."

*   *   *

It was so hot, and so late in the afternoon, that the neighbors were coming down to swim. Mrs. and Mr. Keswick spread their towels, and Gran, and Shelah from across the road, and Kay and Bill from next door. They all admired Pinny, and Becca with her black parasol, and then they went into the water. Becca stayed behind while they swam and chatted.

When they came out, Shelah offered to babysit.

"Really?" Becca asked.

"Really! Go on — you need to cool off."

Shelah sat by Pinny, talking to her in a soft, funny voice.

Becca plunged into the green sea, eyes open, face down. She had to stay where she could touch, but she could dive now, and see under water. She swam along looking at the sand where sunshine rippled like the marks on the seal's skin.

At last she poked her head out of the water, and that's when she saw it — the round head of a grown seal, still as a mooring buoy on a calm day. It turned its face toward her, slipped under water and disappeared.

"Wait!" Becca cried. She looked up at the seal pup, now half in the water, and Shelah nearby talking to Kay and Mrs. Keswick.

The seal mother surfaced again, this time closer to shore. She turned her dark head this way and that, silent.

Becca held her breath. Who would tell Pinny? Why on earth had she decided to leave at this exact moment?

But the baby seal knew. All in an instant Becca glimpsed silver, the sure beat of a strong swimming body. A shadow flitted and they were gone.

"Goodbye, Pinny!" Becca called, and at the same moment, she knew —

"They're here!" she shouted to Gran, splashing out of the water and up the beach, dripping and crying and laughing, stumbling over stone and driftwood.

There was her own mother, and her father behind, holding something in his arms, coming through the trees and on to the beach. Here was her mother's warmth, damp now and salty with tears and the sea from Becca's own skin, and Gran laughing and her father's bright smile, and someone else — her very own, her very first sister, looking up into her face with dark, newborn eyes.

"What shall we call her?" Mum asked.

"Pinny," Becca said.

10. Best Garden

〜〜〜〜〜〜〜〜〜〜〜〜〜〜〜〜〜〜〜〜

Pinny was a warm, solid bundle of digestive noises and sleepiness. Her tufty hair was just the color of the shadowy marks on the seal baby.

"I'm sorry I didn't get here in time to see the baby seal. I would have loved that," Mum said the next morning as she and Becca rocked baby Pin to sleep.

"Now that Pin and your mum and dad are here, it would be helpful if you'd take over watering the garden," Gran told Becca. "I'll show you how to go about it, and you can be responsible."

"I know how to do it already," Becca said. "I've watched you and I've watched Kay."

"Well, some of the neighbors don't like having kids up there without adults, so we have to make sure you know what you're doing just to calm their twitchiness," said Gran. "They have this *thing* about their vegetables. And about their fruits and flowers, too."

Becca knew. Last summer, Mrs. Hughes had yelled at

her for half an hour and all Becca had done was pick one of Gran's daisies. Mrs. Hughes hadn't recognized Becca and had accused her of being one of those wild, destructive children from across the bay. Becca had been kind of interested in the wild children, but when she asked about it Mrs. Hughes went red in the face and stormed off, swinging her hoe with such energy that she whacked the heads off all Rosses' dahlias.

Becca hoped Mrs. Hughes wasn't up there today.

This morning, in the plots that belonged to Henges, Hugheses, Rosses, Keswicks and Toninos, Becca saw poppies and larkspur, lilies and black-eyed susans, feverfew, dahlias, sea holly, bee balm and hollyhocks flowering madly. She saw hefty tomato plants, towering pole beans and bush beans as thick as shrubbery. The neighbors' steady campaign against thistles and buttercups, against slugs, black spot, drought and rust had been a success.

She looked longingly at Rosses' beans. They climbed so far up their poles that even Dr. Ross couldn't reach them. Hedges of pea vines twined upward, looking as though they'd head right into the sky like Jack's beanstalk. Carrots swelled from the earth, just asking to be pulled and eaten.

Becca wasn't allowed to pull anything, of course. She was only allowed to snack from Gran's garden, which meant a nibble of rosemary, maybe, but never a carrot because there weren't any.

"I try but I've no knack for carrots," Gran said.

"Between worms and carrot fly. Never mind. You can't grow everything."

The Rosses had a flower patch, too, full of the red spiky dahlias that looked like sea urchins. They were growing them for the summer fair, and the Hugheses were growing raspberries. Their raspberry canes dripped with berries as big as Becca's thumbs.

"They won't notice if we take one each," Gran muttered. "Nobody's looking."

"Delectable," she said, when she'd picked the seeds from her teeth. "But you mustn't take things when I'm not here. Only if the gardeners offer. And always, always close the gate so the deer can't get in."

"I know."

Frank walked in front of them, leading the way. He sniffed at the roots of Kay's sweetpeas. Becca pushed her face in among the blossoms and breathed in sweetness.

"Why can't we grow stuff like this?"" she mumbled, her head in the flowers.

She knew the answer. Seaweed — that's why Kay's garden was so terrific. Plump, sweet carrots and beets, lettuces bigger than Becca's head and all curly grew in neat plots. Tomatoes were staked like young trees and ripening fruit cascaded from them.

"What we have is lovely," Gran retorted. "I've never tasted rosemary as good as mine!"

"It's the seaweed mulch that makes Kay's garden so good," Becca said.

"I don't believe in all that seaweed," Gran said sharply. "Too much salt! It's bad for the garden."

"But — "

Becca stood staring at Gran's plot and wondered what she could say.

"It's better than last year," she said finally. "Some of the plants are still alive."

"You're getting more like your Aunt Fifi every day," Gran said. "And I don't say that as a compliment. What's wrong with the nasturtiums? They look pretty good, don't they?"

Nasturtium leaves as big as dinner plates surged up among the spindly tomato plants like a green, swelling sea. Maybe that's what had stunted the tomatoes.

"Do you think our tomato will ever ripen?" Becca asked, but Gran just went on to point out, for the tenth time that summer, her eight different kinds of lavender.

"It's drought resistant," she boasted.

Becca didn't know what her gardening father would say after all his hard work. And hers, too, and Alicia's and Lucy's. One tomato, possibly the smallest in the world, no peas at all, bush beans brown and crotchety-looking. Carrots as thin as pins. A healthy crop of thistles and those giant dandelions with prickly leaves. Beets struggling out of the hard earth. It made you want to cry just to look at them.

"I don't have the knack for beets," Gran said. "But we'll keep watering them and hope they come along. The greens are delicious on their own."

Beet greens? thought Becca. More like beet yellows.

"The rosemary does look good," she said, trying to find something nice to say without actually lying.

Gran beamed. "It's massive, isn't it? And look!" She pointed to the climbing beans. "Painted ladies and scarlet emperors."

"Good names," Becca said. She peeked under the leaves, but not a bean did she see.

"They're still developing," Gran explained quickly, and dribbled water at the roots.

Kay's garden was a good bet for the summer fair's Best Garden, but Gran's couldn't compete in any of the usual categories — fruit, flower or vegetable.

"I won Biggest Slug once," Gran said. "Now, do you think you have enough instruction to take over the watering?"

She had told Becca about the plants, explained how to refill the water barrel by connecting the hose at the community well, and described what she called the neighbors' "anxieties." Becca wasn't to go near the Toninos' or the Keswicks' plots, or even breathe on the Hugheses'. But Kay wouldn't mind if Becca went in to smell the sweetpeas now and then.

"I'll do fine by myself," Becca said. She dipped the watering can into the barrel.

Gran left. "Don't forget to bring Frank back," she said. "I think he's chasing snakes in the Keswicks' plot."

Becca sloshed water on the tomatoes. She knew from watching Dad that they needed a lot. She sloshed it on the beans, and tried to thin the desperate, wormy carrots after she gave them a long drink.

When she'd finished watering, she found the clippers and dead-headed Gran's daisies, enjoying the snip-snip of the clippers and the way dried-up flower heads fell to the earth. She'd always wanted to use the snips, but no one would let her. Now that she was chief gardener, she could do what she liked. And that might mean putting a little seaweed here and there, no matter what Gran said.

When she'd finished her chores she looked for Frank. She even looked for him in the plots where she wasn't supposed to go, but she couldn't find him anywhere.

She put the clippers away and made sure the lid was on the water barrel. She collected the weeds she'd pulled and the dead daisies and thinned carrots and took them with her. She opened the gate, let it thump closed behind her, and threw the weeds on the weed pile. That was that. And she would do it all again tomorrow.

When she got home, Frank was in his favorite place by the stove. He must have come home with Gran after all.

* * *

In the morning she went off to borrow Kay's wheelbarrow.

"I don't want to use Gran's," she said. "I don't want to have to explain."

"I won't say a word," said Kay. "You'll find there's a

good drift of seaweed on the beach near Mac's place. I suggest you start there."

It didn't take as long as Becca thought it would, and Mac helped her get the wheelbarrow up off the beach and on to the road.

"You could do with a little help," he said. "Although I don't know any other kid your age who is so into gardening."

"It doesn't matter anyway," said Becca. "There aren't any kids my age around here, into gardening or not into gardening. Anyway, it's not the gardening so much, it's the plants. They deserve a chance, don't you think?"

"I guess they do," Mac said, looking thoughtful.

Becca turned and pushed the wheelbarrow up the road, sweating all the way.

* * *

"Mr. Keswick stopped by," Gran said later. "He brought a posy of sweetpeas for Pin and your mum, and he said something has been nibbling his lettuce plants. Did you see anything when you were up there? He said someone has been barrowing, and he thought the gate might have been open for a while."

Becca stopped still between bites of tomato sandwich.

"No. No, I didn't see any deer. Just slugs."

"Did you squish them?"

"No." She had done it once, but watching the guts come out was disgusting. It reminded her of what it was like to have a very, very bad cold. Besides, she felt awful murdering slugs, even if they were garden pests.

"Anyway, why shouldn't they eat, too?" she asked. "It doesn't seem fair."

* * *

The carrots liked Becca thinning and watering them. Some of them started to grow. And the beet yellows were on their way to becoming greens, suddenly. The clumps of seaweed Becca had put around the plants were keeping the moisture in the earth, at least.

"See? I followed your advice," Becca told Kay. "But don't tell Gran. She doesn't approve."

"It's looking much better," Kay said on her way home from picking tomatoes. "Here, have a tomato."

Becca continued her watering. When she left she let the deer gate bang closed and dumped her weeds on the pile outside. Then she went off to get another load of seaweed.

* * *

In the evening Gran came to her with a troubled face.

"Mrs. Tonino says something ate her beans down to nubs," she said. "Nothing but sticks left, poking out. Her prize beans! Becca, are you sure you remembered to close the gate?"

"I know I did," Becca said. "I heard it thump, and I looked at it, too."

"Did you see anything?" asked Gran.

"Nope."

For a moment, Gran's face wavered.

"Are you sure?"

"I'm sure! Why do you have to keep asking? I'm sure! I'm sure! I'm sure I closed the gate!"

"Did it thump? Did you check it?"

Becca didn't know what to say. Why had Gran asked her to look after the garden in the first place if she didn't think she was able to close the gate, even?

"It's just — " Gran began.

Becca had to leave the room then. She went down to the beach and kicked a piece of driftwood. Was she going crazy? But she remembered closing the gate quite clearly.

*   *   *

After that she was even more hugely careful. But in the next few days Mrs. Tonino lost half her radishes and Mr. Hughes was ranting about his cosmos being chewed up, along with his broccoli. But that, Becca thought, hadn't been doing so well in the first place, being all leaves and stalks and almost none of the broccoli-ish bits. And anyway, who would want to grow something that tasted like — well, she wasn't even going to bother to think it. It made oyster stew look really good.

"I don't approve of children having gardening responsibilities," Mr. Hughes growled at Becca when he saw her working on Gran's plot. She was on the fourth load of seaweed by then. "I don't think they should be in here at all."

"Becca's as careful as you are," said Kay as she tended her lilies. "Maybe it's a possum. Or a rare aggressive plant disease."

"Humpf," said Mr. Hughes. "Possums don't eat broccoli. It has the chew marks of a rampaging deer. And that could only be because someone didn't close the gate!"

He glared at Becca.

Becca pressed her lips together and went to look for Frank. Maybe he was eating the vegetables, but it didn't seem likely. Becca had offered him spinach once and he had turned around and mooned her.

He wasn't to be found in the garden — again.

"Have you seen Frank?" she asked Kay. "I brought him in with me and he's disappeared."

"Probably chewing at Mr. Hughes' heels," said Kay sympathetically. "Don't listen to him, Becca. You're doing a wonderful job. And the garden has really perked up since you took over. There are no more thistles and it's just possible that your gran'll get a carrot that's thicker than a knitting needle. Here are some rosebuds to take down for you and Pin."

* * *

But the next day, all the buds had been eaten off Kay's rosebush. Every single one.

"I don't see why they blame me," Becca said after Gran hung up the phone.

Mum put Pin in Becca's arms and Pin snuggled there

as if she couldn't care less about chewed rosebuds or bean plants gnawed down to nubs.

"We know you're careful," Mum said. "But maybe Dad or I should do the watering for a couple of days. Mistakes happen, you know."

"Mistakes don't 'happen,'" Becca said. "People make them."

"That's true," said Gran.

Becca looked into Gran's face. Here we go again, she thought. She looked down at Pin instead. Folded up tight in sleep, Pin's face looked like a flower bud itself. It looked like it belonged to a person who wouldn't dream of blaming her sister for something she never would have done.

"Becca —" Mum said.

"Hilary," Gran commanded.

"Well, she's a kid after all," Mum said. "At least the neighbors would stop blaming her. And you."

"Hilary," Gran repeated sternly. "Don't you know your own daughter?"

For a moment she looked dangerous. Now she was actually sticking up for Becca! What would she say when she found out about the seaweed?

"I have to go out," blurted Becca, pushing Pin back into Mum's arms so suddenly that Pin gave a surprised squeak. "I've got something to do."

* * *

She stood in a quiet place under some cedar boughs. After a while, Frank came.

"What do you know?" she asked, as he purred and pushed against her. It was nice to have someone on her side. "What do you know about the garden? That nobody else knows? That grumpy, roaring old Mr. Hughes with his horrible broccoli doesn't know? That even Kay doesn't know? Or the Keswicks or Toninos or even Gran?"

She sat down, hidden by the branches, thinking.

She remembered Frank leading her through the salal to the oaks. Well, she'd just follow him again.

"Lead me there," she muttered into his fur. He shivered all over.

* * *

Frank walked ahead of her as if everything were ordinary. He waited for her to open the gate, and then to stop and breathe in the comforting scent of Gran's scabby Gravenstein apples.

He sat by her as she dipped the watering can into the barrel and watched as she began to water Gran's beanless scarlet emperors and painted ladies.

But in a moment he had disappeared.

Becca put the watering can down. She looked around. There was Frank's tail, twitching slowly in the shrubbery of Mr. Keswick's purple bush beans — or at least, they used to be bush beans. Now they looked like they'd lost a fight. They were lying mauled and broken in the dirt.

"I see you," she whispered to Frank. Maybe he was the one eating the garden.

She sneaked up, treading carefully along the path

between the half-pulled stumps of Mrs. Tonino's radishes and her still-flourishing lettuces.

Frank's tail twitched once more and disappeared. This time Becca spotted his ears, sharp and upright in the Henges' pea patch. But by the time she got there he was gone. And so were some of Henges' peas, and the vines and leaves, too.

"Oh, Frank! What have you done?"

But even as she said that, her eye found him again. His tail was sticking up straight now, a black brush in the middle of the Keswicks' blue sea holly.

And now he was sniffing about in Mr. Hughes' half-eaten broccoli, right up against the fence at the foot of the garden.

With a few stealthy strides, Becca gained on him. If she skirted the tomato plants climbing up their frames near the back fence, she'd be able to catch him.

Who would have guessed? A fruit- and vegetable-eating cat! One who even ate broccoli!

She squeezed around the end of the tomato stakes. Right up near Becca's shoulders, broken tomato blossoms dangled and the raw wounds of torn branches showed pale among the green.

How had Frank managed that?

There he was, peering down the row of jungly plants. She could nab him if she was quiet and fast. His hindquarters were high, his eyes intent, and his tail switched back and forth, the way it did when he was stalking.

And he *was* stalking. Before Becca could step out from behind the tomatoes, something happened.

A head appeared.

And it wasn't the head of a cat.

It was a deer! A full-grown one, with antlers branching beautifully and a long, delicate face.

Beautiful, delicate, and a marauder.

Becca stood stock still and the deer snaked through a gap in the fence, pushing the wire back from the post as it went. Watched by Becca on one side and Frank on the other, it unfolded itself, lifted its head of antlers high, twitched its ears and stepped up to lunch on Mr. Hughes' tomatoes.

* * *

After the fence had been mended, all the neighbors stopped by to thank Becca. Some even apologized.

Mr. Hughes gave Becca a big bunch of beets in thanks.

"It would have been broccoli, but it's chewed to bits," he said, and Becca looked at Gran.

"A victim of the deer smorgasbord!" Gran said cheerfully. She knew how Becca felt about broccoli.

"I knew it couldn't have been your fault, really," said Kay, offering Becca a bouquet of sweetpeas. "But I did just doubt for a moment and I'm sorry. I should have known you'd never leave the gate open, just from seeing the way you took care of your gran's garden."

"Our garden." Gran smiled.

"The Best Garden," said Kay, "as it turns out! What do

you think, Isobel? It's an historic occasion. Not having a thing that interested the deer, you triumphed. And it was thanks to Becca. And the seaweed!"

"Seaweed!" Gran exclaimed. "What seaweed?"

11. The Chimney

~~~~~~

THE GARDEN affair died down, but people continued to bring Becca vegetables and flowers. As she lugged yet another basket overflowing with zucchini, carrots and bright dahlias down from the garden, she had to stop in Gran's driveway to rest her arms.

Suddenly, with a swish and a crunch on the stones, there was Aunt Fifi, pulling up in her sporty car.

"I'm back!" she announced, jumping out to give Becca a hug. "Here for the grand celebrations. How are things going? How's Mac's cabin coming along? What's with the good-looking garden stuff? That's surely not Mum's!"

Becca told her everything, including not just the rampaging deer and the whole seaweed standoff, but also the situation with Mr. Hughes' broccoli. It had somehow revived in the days since the fence had been fixed.

"He keeps bringing bunches of it over," she complained. "And Gran cooks it and Mum keeps saying I should eat it and it smells like — well, you know! I hate it."

"Hmm," said Aunt Fifi, looking at her for a long while.

"There are too many adults around," said Becca. "And now there are going to be even more. Along with cousins who only want to be grouchy or read."

The whole family was gathering for Pin's official welcome to the world.

"Well, as adults and cousins go they could be worse, believe me!" Aunt Fifi consoled her, as they headed down the path to the cabin.

"Aunt Fifi's the vanguard," said Gran gloomily. "I don't know how we're going to manage for water when everyone gets here. And the island's dry as tinder. It could go up in smoke any time."

The combination of seaweed in the garden and having to prepare the house for so many visitors had sent Gran into a funk.

Fifi gave her a great hug. "Don't worry, Mum! It'll be okay. And look at Becca! She's changed since I last saw her — definitely looks like a sister! And Hilary!" she cried, dropping her pack. "And baby Pin!"

For a moment Aunt Fifi's face became tender and wondering as she held the bundle that was Pin, and looked for the first time into Pin's face.

"Is it true you sang her out of the sea?" she asked Becca.

"Not really," said Becca, "but the seal pup and Pin arrived the same day. And I took care of them both."

"It's like Shakespeare," said Aunt Fifi, "when a sister

and a brother both wash up on to the shore of a fantastical country. Which reminds me…"

"Have you seen Merlin?" Becca whispered.

"Utterly *not*," Aunt Fifi whispered back. "Anyway, he's a confirmed — "

"What?" Becca asked.

"A confirmed… plumber. Which is a good thing!" she added quickly. "But he lives on the island. And…"

"You don't," said Becca. "Oh, too bad. But why couldn't you — "

But Aunt Fifi rushed on with her greetings.

"How are you, Hill?" she asked Mum and Dad, and they both said, "Tired!" at the same time.

"Well, Becca and I will take over now," Aunt Fifi promised. She hugged Becca and Pin, both together in her sun-browned arms.

Everything was lively now that Aunt Fifi was back. Becca watched Gran and saw that she was smiling despite all her dire talk about water and fire hazards.

* * *

"Fifi will probably want to involve you in something dangerous," Gran warned Becca very early the next morning. "She might get it into her head to make another batch of jelly."

"Nothing more dangerous than swimming!" said Aunt Fifi, as she yawned into view and seized a mug of tea. "Did you make this, Becca? It's perfect morning tea."

"Thick enough to stand a spoon in," agreed Gran, coughing.

"That's how I like it," Becca said. "And I like the way the sugar cakes on the bottom, too. I make it this way for Mum when she gets up early to nurse Pin. Pin always wakes us up way before we're ready."

"Well, I'm going back to bed," Gran said. "It's one thing to keep Hilary and Pin company at dawn but I feel a visitation of sleep coming upon me. I think you're a hero to look after your mum in the mornings, Becca. Fifi, watch the fire and make sure it's low before you and Becca head off to swim."

Gran disappeared into her bedroom and Becca and Aunt Fifi sat and drank tea as the sky lightened.

"Are you ready, Becca?" Aunt Fifi asked.

Becca sat on her cold toes. The sun wasn't even really up yet. Plunging into the sea wasn't the first thing on her mind, but swimming before the sun came up might be as interesting as swimming at night.

"I'll build up the fire so we can warm up when we get out," Aunt Fifi said, jumping up to rummage in the woodbox.

"I thought Gran said to leave it low," Becca said.

"Well, she's a little overly cautious, I sometimes think," said Aunt Fifi, grunting as she threw wood about. "Ah, here we go. A nice pitchy log to go in with a piece of alder. That'll give us a fire we could bake bread on."

"But we don't want to bake bread," Becca said.

"We might change our minds," said Aunt Fifi. "Hurry up! Or we won't beat the sun."

*   *   *

There wasn't a soul on the beach.

"The sand is cold," Becca said.

"Yep! The sun hasn't warmed it up yet," Aunt Fifi answered.

"Look at the water! It's so gray! It's the color of nails."

"Pewter," said Aunt Fifi.

But she strode into the frisky, forbidding waves as if it were a sunny afternoon.

"Come on, darling Beck," she said, and threw herself into the sea.

"I'm coming," Becca muttered. She let her feet into the water bit by bit, and the waves splashed up to her shins. When it reached the back of her knees she had to pause, and then finally she made it up to her waist.

"The cabin will be warm when we get back," Aunt Fifi called as she floated. "It's okay if we're a bit chilly now."

Becca looked back at the smoke coming out of Gran's chimney and ducked under the gray sea.

*   *   *

When she came up, the sun was a spot of fire on the margin of the mountains.

"Look!" she cried. Aunt Fifi stopped swimming and together they watched golden sunshine pour forth from an ever-widening round. The sea turned yellow and pink and, in moments, blue and sparkling with light. The day was born.

"Isn't it grand!" Aunt Fifi exclaimed.

And Becca threw handfuls of water into the air and watched it fall back into the sea, sharp with the sun's brilliance.

* * *

"The chimney's smoking nicely now," Becca said as they dripped up from the sea.

"It'll be good and toasty in there," Aunt Fifi said. "I'm just going to have a rinse in the outdoor shower, but you go ahead in."

Becca washed her feet at the back door, then wiped them on the foot towel. She opened the door, and she heard crackling.

"Gran?"

The front room was empty, and warm as toast as Aunt Fifi had predicted.

"Toast," Becca said. "Crackling." She was trying to describe for herself the noises now tickling her eardrums.

She looked at the stove. It wasn't smoking, but it was hot. Really hot. The kettle on the back of it was boiling madly.

But what was crackling? She didn't dare lift the lid to look in the firebox.

The whole stove seemed to vibrate with heat.

"Gran?" she asked again. She walked around to the woodbox behind the stove.

The stovepipe was red and angry-looking. Where it should have been black, it glowed with a dull, fiery seriousness. It sounded as if it were alive, as if it were about to rise up and step into the world.

"Something is wrong," she said out loud.

She couldn't believe what was happening. She had heard about this, from school and her parents. And now here it was — fire!

And she was the only one to know.

Although she couldn't see flames, she could feel them. She could hear them inside the stove and its stovepipe licking away — grasping, whispering in their upward rush. Up at the top of the pipe were the dry cedar planks of Gran's ceiling, perfect kindling. The metal shield that protected them from the hot chimney pipe suddenly looked flimsy and useless.

For a moment it seemed as if the world was still. Aunt Fifi was in the outdoor shower, too far to call. The cabin was full of sleeping family — Mum and Dad, Pin and Gran, all sleeping peacefully, thinking that today Mollie and Ardeth, Auntie Clare and Uncle Clarence would arrive, and Lucy and Alicia and Aunt Meg and Uncle Martin, and that tomorrow they would all celebrate Pin's birthday.

But inside the stovepipe, inside the very cabin where they slept, fire was raging.

What should she do?

"911," she thought, picking up Gran's phone. She looked at her fingers punching in the numbers as if they belonged to someone else — a girl in a movie, perhaps. This couldn't be real.

"Police, fire or ambulance," snapped a voice.

"A fire," Becca said. "It's at Gran's house."

But they didn't want directions about "the third house on Bosun's Bay" and "big tree," which were the only ones Becca could think of.

"Is the fire at the address you're calling from?" the lady interrupted.

"Yes!" And almost before she'd hung up Becca heard the siren soaring faintly from the middle of the island and the firehall.

"Gran!" she called, running into the bedroom. "Get up!"

Her voice was a squeak, as if she couldn't get any air into herself, but even so Gran sat up abruptly and knocked over the glass of water by her bed.

"Darn!" she shouted, still half asleep.

Afterwards Becca remembered that "Darn!" and it made her laugh — Gran's strongest language. But now she just said, "Fire!" and Gran was out of bed in a second. Becca didn't wait to tell her more, but rushed upstairs to the back bedroom, to Mum and Dad.

"Get up!" she said. "The fire guys are coming! Gran's stove is burning up! Get up! Get Pin!"

She rushed to Pin's basket and lifted her out, cuddling her as she stormed downstairs, Mum and Dad close behind her, grabbing up their clothes as they ran.

"We have to take her outside," she cried. "We all have to go outside!"

"Glory, glory," muttered Gran. "And the island's dry as

tinder!" She sat on the back steps and pulled on her shoes, then stepped out to look up at where the chimney pipe rose red from the roof.

"What are you doing?" Aunt Fifi asked, appearing wrapped in a towel and dripping from her shower. "Are we eating breakfast outside?"

"It's a fire!" Becca shouted, clutching Pin. "It's a fire!"

The siren rose to a painful shriek. Seconds later, Merlin and his fire fighters came pouring down the trail.

* * *

Mum and Gran stood about in their nightclothes, and Pin in her sleeper nestled in Dad's arms. Aunt Fifi was still wrapped in her bath towel, hair dripping, her face pale with shock.

After he had checked the house, and clanking a bit in his fire chief's outfit, Merlin took Becca back into the cabin.

"It's very easy to deal with a chimney fire," he explained quietly. "If you get it early, like you did, even a small cup of water will usually do. Just throw the water right into the firebox and put the lid back on, and steam will drown the flames."

He showed her how to do it, then looked at her seriously. She burst into tears.

"You did absolutely the right thing," he said kindly, hugging her to all his buckles and fire-fighting implements. "You are an absolute, amazing hero." Then his voice went a little grim. "But I'll have to have a talk with your gran and Fifi."

Now that the danger was over, the rest of the fire fighters milled about exchanging chimney-fire stories and admiring Pin. Mrs. Barker took off her fire fighter's hat and gave Pin a kiss.

But Becca heard Merlin talk gravely to Gran about the state of her chimney.

"But I've just been having tiny fires to burn the rubbish," Gran said apologetically. "I've been so worried about the fire hazard that I've hardly used the wood stove at all."

"It's a common mistake," Merlin said. "But it's those little fires that gummed up the lower part of the stovepipe. And Fifi — "

"I know," said Aunt Fifi. She was pink in the face, and it wasn't just because she was standing in the middle of a crew of fire fighters wearing nothing but a towel. "I didn't listen to my mother! She told me not to build up the fire, and I did. And that pitchy wood burns so hot."

For a moment her face looked pained and then she covered it with her hand.

It was strange to see Aunt Fifi acting like a kid in trouble. Becca went over and took her hand.

"You just wanted us to be warm," she said. "And it was a wonderful swim."

"At least it burned out the creosote messing up the stovepipe," Gran said to Merlin, and something about her voice made Becca rush over to her.

"Here — sit down," Becca said, opening out a beach chair. Gran sank into it in a most un-Gran-like way, almost as if she didn't have the strength to stand any longer.

"Isobel, it's the worst possible way to clean your chimney," Merlin admonished her. "And Fifi — " He gave her a long look. "Be careful," he said, managing to sound ferocious and gentle at once.

Then he rounded up the fire fighters and they all trooped back up to the road, carrying their unused rolled-up hose, hatchets and extinguishers, and whistling. Becca heard the great fire truck roar back up to the fire hall, not needed. Thank goodness.

Kay and Bill fed them breakfast on their deck. Kay had made muffins, and she brought out two kinds of homemade cookies. Becca had coffee for the first time and that was very interesting.

And she had never seen Bill in his pajamas before. That was interesting, too, because there was such a big tear around one of the sleeves that she could see his hairy armpit quite clearly.

"Let's hope Pin's birthday festivities are less alarming," said Gran. "When we get around to them."

"They might be," said Becca, grinning to herself as she dumped another spoon of sugar in her coffee. "And then again, they might not. I invited Merlin to the party."

12. Island Birthday

~~~~~~

"I DON'T care whether or not Becca invited Merlin," came Aunt Fifi's voice from the deck. "I refuse to go with him in Arnulf's boat. I simply don't trust that man in a boat. He couldn't tie a bowline to save his life."

Becca thought Aunt Fifi was just feeling grumpy about yesterday's near-disaster.

"Why *did* you invite Merlin?" Gran asked Becca as they checked out the Zodiac's *chambres flottantes* in preparation for Pin's birthday excursion over to Camas Island. "It's not like we don't have enough family drama without him. Things could go bust at any minute! Meg and Martin, Lucy and Alicia, Mollie and Ardeth, Clare and Clarence, your mum and dad... we're very argumentative when we all get together. You know that. It's probably a good thing Catriona's on call and couldn't come."

"I thought Aunt Fifi might want to start a fire," Becca said. "Wouldn't it be safer to have him around? Anyway, I like him."

"Well, you've certainly done a fine job of arranging the party," Gran said. "It should be a very dynamic crew. Is there anyone else you've invited without telling me?"

"Yep. I invited Mac, too. He's nice, and he could teach me how to kayak."

"Mac! But he's not even coming to the island until late today. He has to work."

"What *is* his work?" Becca asked. "Anyway, I told him he had to come, and he promised."

"You're very commanding these days," said Gran, but then she suddenly gave a command herself.

"Heave!"

Becca hefted her side of the Zodiac, and she and Gran carried the boat down to the sea.

Right behind them came Dad with the canoe on his head. Auntie Clare and Uncle Clarence followed with a load of beach towels, birthday presents, bathing suits, picnic baskets and a cooler.

"Becca, did you phone Dugald?" Dad asked, his voice muffled by the canoe.

"Winds variable five to ten knots," Becca reported. But she kept to herself the rest of what Dugald had said — "Rising to northwest twenty to twenty-five knots in the late afternoon."

She knew if she said anything Gran wouldn't want to go, and it had been Becca's idea that they celebrate Pin's birthday on Camas Island. It might be her only trip there this summer.

* * *

"It's a fleet!" Becca said, looking back. She, Gran, Mollie and Ardeth were zooming ahead in the Zodiac.

"Look at them!" Mollie exclaimed. "Uncle Martin's going to capsize that thing if he doesn't stop horsing around. Why doesn't he sit down?"

For Uncle Martin had decided to sail the *Glaucous Gull* once more, despite the light winds. Auntie Meg and Lucy and Alicia were there to help him.

"Lucy and Alicia might get stuck rowing," Becca shouted over the buzz of the motor.

They could see Lucy and Alicia arguing with Uncle Martin as the *Glaucous Gull* dropped farther and farther behind the rest of the family. Auntie Meg drooped in the bow, looking a bit the way Uncle Martin had on that first rough voyage.

"Auntie Meg doesn't look too good," Ardeth reported after inspecting her with the binoculars. "And it isn't even rough. She probably wishes she'd come with us."

"Or with Mum." Becca thought of Mum with Pin in the baby backpack, having a quiet stroll through the forest to the beach where she and Gran would pick them up and ferry them over to Camas Island.

Dad and Auntie Clare were making good time with their paddles. Uncle Clarence was lounging amidships in a nest of life jackets and birthday presents. Becca could see him gesturing with his hands, probably telling Dad all about their work in clinics in Africa.

Aunt Fifi was paddling Mac's kayak. To Becca it had seemed a weird coincidence that when Merlin had appeared, just in the nick of time before they all pushed off, he'd brought a kayak instead of his brother-in-law's boat.

"Arnulf hasn't recovered from my account of the last time," he confided to Becca. "Anyway, simple is best. I just got this second-hand. Good, isn't it?"

Proudly he had displayed his new find — a kayak for two.

"You have to watch out for second-hand boats," Becca had said and wondered if Aunt Fifi would possibly consent to paddle a kayak with Merlin.

"I value my independence," Aunt Fifi said when Becca suggested it. But independent or not, Becca noticed now that Merlin and her aunt were paddling side by side. And Aunt Fifi was actually laughing.

It was sunny and hot on Camas Island. Uncle Martin and Auntie Clare constructed a driftwood shelter so Pin could sleep in the shade, and Mum and Auntie Meg sat in it together while Mum nursed Pin.

"It's the best, Meg," Mum was saying. "Becca and Pin. For me not having them would be like never leaving my hometown."

It was strange what adults said to one another when they thought no one was listening. Becca crunched along the pebbles, watching. Auntie Clare, Dad and Gran were down at the water's edge, carefully lifting stones to see what lay beneath.

"Hillel," she heard Gran say to Dad from the middle of a tide pool, "come and look here. A nudibranch I've never seen before."

Up in the middle of the island, Uncle Martin and Uncle Clarence were walking through the dry, golden grasses, peering up at the light that rose far above them. Their voices floated back to Becca, a rise and fall of sound with no words.

"Well, I think Becca's too young to do it," she suddenly heard Alicia declare.

"I am not!" Becca said loudly.

She stumped over a rise in the beach to find all four of them lolling in the driftwood.

"I am not too young! To do what?"

"Swim around Camas Island," Lucy said. "Alicia and I've been wanting to forever. Anyway, I don't think you're too young. You got us home from the middle of that forest, didn't you?"

"Yes, I did," Becca said, looking fiercely at Alicia. Looking at her reminded Becca of the fine, silvery trees and the wish she had made there.

"And she saved the whole family from the chimney fire," Ardeth pointed out.

"And she's gone skinny-swimming with the falling stars," said Mollie.

"And I drove the Zodiac all by myself through the herring run," said Becca.

"She was kissed by a seal!" Lucy exclaimed. "Gran said."

"Don't get so mad," said Alicia. "It's a long way! And the water's cold. And you're just not used to swimming that far."

"I can do it," Becca insisted.

"Sure you can," Mollie said. "You're a night swimmer! You won't be scared of what's swimming around underneath you."

For a second Becca paused. This wouldn't be the safe, familiar bay with its floor of silver sand. Out here in the strait was where the wild creatures traveled — orcas and seals and the rowdy sea lions she and Gran had seen barking their heads off in spring, not to mention the schools of tiny herring there must be rushing about after all that spawning that went on in the spring.

"We'll get Aunt Fifi and Merlin to come with us in the kayaks," Ardeth said. "So if one of us gets tired they can haul us into shore."

* * *

"I'd like to swim, too," Aunt Fifi said. "How about we get Gran and the other aunts to come in the boats?"

So Becca found herself swimming between Aunt Fifi and Ardeth, while Mollie, Lucy and Alicia forged on ahead. Auntie Meg and Mum paddled Merlin's kayak, and Gran and Aunt Clare floated along in the canoe.

"Look at them." She heard Merlin's voice from the shore. "They make an outstanding flock. Or should I say pod?"

Up on the beach, Dad, Merlin and the uncles cheered.

* * *

"We'll go with the current at first," Aunt Fifi said. "Stay close to shore so you just get the edge of it, though. You don't want to be swept out into the strait."

With every stroke the tidal current zoomed Becca forward. Down below, green seaweed and old oyster shells fairly whizzed by.

"You want to try some crawl?" Ardeth asked, so Becca put in her face and pulled away at the water, kicking hard. The bottom dropped away and all she could see beneath her was shadow.

When she turned her head to breathe, Aunt Fifi was right there.

In a few minutes they rounded the first point. Becca switched to breaststroke.

"They're way ahead of us," she said to Ardeth and Aunt Fifi.

Aunt Fifi plunged along calmly.

"No matter," she said. "It's not a race…"

"Time to swim on my back," Becca said.

She stared up into the blue sky, flutter-kicking madly. Now if she turned her head she could see the grassy banks on this side of the island. On top of one of them Dad was holding Pin, watching Becca's progress. Merlin was beside him.

She waved.

"How are you holding up?" came Mum's voice and Gran's almost at the same time.

"She looks great," said Auntie Meg. "A selkie."

"Are you getting tired?" asked Mum.

"Cold?" asked Gran.

Both, Becca could have said. But she just smiled wetly.

"I'm okay," she told them and kicked her feet with as much energy as she could.

If she looked eastward, she could see far across the strait, all the way to the coastal mountains rising up snowy and sharp on the mainland. The sea felt huge. And it was dark underneath.

Pull… pull… pull… Her arms ached, and she was starting to feel like she had frog legs. They just kept doing frog-kick, over and over again.

"It's getting shallower," Ardeth said. "Look, you can see the bottom again."

They were almost at the south end of Camas Island. Now they'd have to swim through the shallow channel between the island and the sea-lion rocks, where today seals lay about in the summer sun.

Lucy and Alicia were waiting for them, and Mollie was, too.

"This is a cinch," said Alicia.

"So what are you waiting for?" Aunt Fifi asked.

"Oh, we just thought we'd go with you through the seal channel," Alicia said, looking at Becca. "In case somebody needs help."

Becca floated on her back to rest, sneaking peeks at the reefs that were covered with seals. She remembered the moment she'd come face to face with the seal. She remembered Pinny flying through the water to join her mother. From here the seals just looked like a lot of lumps, but she knew what they were like in the water. Sleek and powerful and really not human.

Becca looked at her. Alicia didn't have a clue.

"Should we go on?" asked Mum and Gran and the aunts. Mollie and Ardeth, Lucy and Alicia watched her.

"Yes," she said, and her frog legs started kicking again.

In the shallow channel, the water was running against them.

Kick… pull… kick… pull…

The seals on the reef turned their heads.

Alicia and Lucy were right behind her.

"Will they come after us?" Lucy puffed.

"Don't be dumb," Alicia said. "Just keep swimming."

Becca didn't say a word. She looked at the seals out of the corner of her eye.

Suddenly, it felt like she and Lucy and Alicia were all alone. Even though Mollie and Ardeth and Aunt Fifi were swimming not far behind them, and Gran and the aunts and Mum were in the boats behind that, it seemed like they might not be there at all. And the water was the seals' home, and she was a visitor here.

"Well, this isn't so bad," Alicia said loudly. "This isn't *so* terrifying."

At the sound of her voice dozens of seals poked up their heads. They turned dark eyes and whiskered faces to the girls.

"Just swim," Becca whispered. "And shut up."

"I'm not scared," Alicia insisted. "They can come into the water, for all I care."

Becca looked back. The seals were still watching them.

Bit by bit, the shore passed by. The current in the channel weakened, then disappeared as they rounded the corner and headed along the western shore, swimming into choppy waves that slapped up into Becca's face.

In a few minutes the seals were out of sight.

"Why was that so weird?" she wondered.

"I don't know," Lucy answered. "It felt scary."

"You guys are wimpy," Alicia declared.

"It's stupid not to be nervous," Becca puffed as she continued her breaststroke. She remembered what it had been like to have sea lions hurling themselves about only an oar's length away. They didn't care about people.

Alicia snorted, but maybe she was just coughing sea that had gone up her nose. Aunt Fifi and Mollie and Ardeth caught up to them then. Becca could see Dad with Pin, and Merlin with Uncle Martin up on the beach. Merlin's hat blew off and he had to run after it, and Uncle Martin was waving his arms about something and looking agitated.

But Becca kept swimming. Her lungs hurt now, and her throat was sore with seawater she'd accidently swallowed. Her arms and legs felt flabby and dead, and somehow it seemed harder to swim than it had been.

"Do you want a tow?" Gran asked.

"No," Becca coughed as she tried to breathe. She had sucked in a great slop of sea.

Mollie, Lucy and Alicia were in front again now, and even Ardeth had decided to swim ahead. Only Aunt Fifi remained by her side.

"Martin and Merlin seem to be having a little fit about something," Aunt Fifi observed. "How like Merlin to start a fight at a sunny afternoon picnic."

"Fifi!" Gran exclaimed.

"Mark my words," was all Aunt Fifi would say. "How are you doing, Becca?"

Becca gasped.

"Fine," she meant to say, but nothing came out.

She turned on her back again, but water kept washing over her head so she had to switch back to her front.

"Do you want a tow?" Aunt Fifi asked, as Mum and Auntie Meg paddled up beside them.

Becca wished they'd stop asking.

"Okay," said Aunt Fifi. "I'll just swim along beside you and you can grab me if you need to. Mother, I've been thinking a great deal about the garden," she went on, puffing every once in a while as she took another stroke. "It's clear from Becca's enormous success with it, this being the very first year in recorded history that the garden has rendered up a carrot thicker than a baby's finger, that you are going to have to revise your policy on that all-important issue, *seaweed mulch*."

"I didn't mean to start a fight!" Becca panted.

"You know what I think about seaweed and the garden," Gran said, ignoring Becca. "I wasn't going to make a big fuss about it, and Becca did work very hard, but there's too much salt in seaweed and how do you know it won't leach through the soil and pollute the well?"

"Oh, I didn't think of that!" Becca tried to say, but Aunt Fifi was already talking.

"Kay and the others all agree that that is utter — " Here a wave must have slapped into Aunt Fifi's face, for Becca couldn't hear the next word. "In any case I brought along a file of articles about the benefits of seaweed mulch," she went on. "All very scientific. Why don't you just stop being so pig-headed for once, exercise your reason, and come around to a right way of thinking? And anyway it would be cruel — cruel! — not to build on the great progress Becca has made. Becca! Who actually knows that plants need more than a thimbleful of water every two days!"

"Fifi!" shouted Mum, Auntie Meg and Aunt Clare all at the same time.

"Oh, sorry, Mum," said Aunt Fifi cheerfully. "Don't mean to be rude! What I mean is, how about giving it a go for a while? And it would be nice for Becca, too, after all the work she's put in. Right, Becca?"

Becca didn't know whether she wanted to answer or not.

"You won't find enough seaweed on the beach at this time of year anyway," said Gran, panting with the effort of paddling. "And exactly who is going to cart it all the way up from the beach to the garden? I'd like to know. Not you! You're far too busy with your blackberry pies and all-night arguments with the only plumber on the island, not to mention — "

Suddenly Becca realized that they'd arrived back at the beach they'd started from. There were Alicia and Lucy, Mollie and Ardeth staggering out of the water like sea creatures not used to land life.

Mum and Auntie Meg beached the kayak and Gran jumped out of the bow of the canoe to pull it up on shore. Aunt Fifi and Becca swam in slowly, carried by the waves that washed them up on to the pebbles, surging and sucking by turns.

I made it, Becca thought, lying face down on the clean, sea-washed rocks. Hugging the land. She turned her head and looked straight into Aunt Fifi's face.

"How come you started talking about seaweed all of a sudden?" she asked.

"Why shouldn't I talk about seaweed if I want to?" Aunt Fifi said. "What — now we can't even bring up the subject, never mind do anything about it?"

But she looked enormously pleased.

It was as Becca had guessed. The whole argument hadn't been about seaweed, really. It had been Aunt Fifi's way of helping Becca finish the swim, and maybe even Gran's, too.

*   *   *

"Hurrah for the circumnavigators!" cried Merlin, Dad and the uncles.

Uncle Clarence took pictures of all the swimmers together, then all the swimmers and paddlers.

"How about getting one of all the cousins?" asked Gran. "I like to see my grandchildren all lined up together."

"I never thought you'd make it," Alicia said to Becca. "But you did! Maybe next year we can swim around the big island. What do you think?"

"How about standing by this log?" Uncle Clarence asked. "You can line up by height."

Becca pressed against Lucy's wet arm, shivering even though she was holding Pin in a bundle of blankets. Just as Uncle Clarence snapped the pictures, she felt the touch of something warm and fleecy — Auntie Meg slipping quickly in between photos to put her jacket over Becca and Pin.

"Look out to sea and smile!" Uncle Clarence commanded.

Becca did. Her wet hair stuck clammily to her head, and the boisterous northwest wind of Dugald's small-craft warning blew straight into her face.

* * *

Long, long after they had all arrived back at Gran's, after the blowy picnic of deviled eggs and shortbread biscuits and birthday cake and stinky cheese that Merlin had insisted she try, Becca sat alone and thought about the day. But it wasn't Alicia being mean and then practically inviting her to swim around the big island that stayed in her mind. It wasn't being surrounded by aunts and cousins as she swam all the way around Camas Island and the uncles. It wasn't the happy moment of Pin's birthday presents, made hugely better by Auntie Meg and Uncle Martin's "welcome to sisterhood" present for Becca — a really good mask and snorkel.

Nor was it what she had noticed about the photograph Uncle Clarence had taken — that there had stood Ardeth, then Mollie, and beside Mollie Alicia, and then Lucy, all wet and shivery, and then Becca with Pin in her arms — the end of the line. But she hadn't been the end of the line, after all. Suddenly, Auntie Meg had appeared with a jacket, and she had stayed there while the camera went click.

There was another cousin in the picture, Becca had realized then. One that was even smaller than Pin. One you couldn't see yet because she was still growing inside Auntie Meg.

But even that wasn't what stuck most in Becca's mind. What she remembered best was the rescue — the way Aunt Fifi and Merlin had kayaked valiantly back to the big island when the wind blew up too hard for the little boats to get back, and had commandeered Arnulf's boat, but this time with Mac to pilot it.

And Mac had come. He had come with the weather at his heels, full of accounts of frontal systems and high-pressure ridges and small-craft warnings, because he had come straight from his work as a weatherman.

And not just any weatherman, either.

"Did you know?" Becca asked Gran. "Mac is Dugald! No wonder his voice always sounded so familiar!"

But Gran had just smiled and said, "He's brought something else, too, besides weather reports."

And up from the hold in the boat popped a head, a figure in an orange life jacket.

"Guess what!" Mac told Becca as he helped her into Arnulf's boat.

"What?" Becca said. "And who's that?"

"I'm a great-uncle!" Mac said. "And this is Jane, my great-niece who is visiting. And she is very, very good with a wheelbarrow. Has been practicing, in fact."

Jane! Her hair stuck out and she had scabs on both knees and a hole where one of her teeth should have been.

"It wasn't a baby tooth," she told Becca. "I got it when I rode into a tree on my bike. I wanted to see how far I could go with my eyes closed without crashing. Did you really swim all the way around the island? And save your family from a burning house?"

"Well, sort of," Becca said.

"What are you going to do next?"

"Actually, next I want to hike around the big island," Becca told her, as they crouched in the bottom of the boat. "We could take a backpack and a ton of food and…"

"Yes!" said Jane. "And when we get home, we can go swimming in the dark."

"Skinny-dipping! And watch the falling stars," said Becca.

"We can sleep on the point by ourselves," said Jane.

"We can do a play," said Becca. "Aunt Fifi and Merlin can help."

"We can get Uncle Mac to teach us to kayak."

"We can go sailing!"

"We can sail around the big island," said Jane. "Or sail and sleep over on Camas Island."

"I'll show you the oak forest — " said Becca. Then she stopped still, remembering a long-ago wish whispered into warm bark.

It's come true. It's really come true, she thought, while Arnulf's boat made its way through the dusk and the evening waves, and behind them the light of Camas Island blinked steadily, faithfully, in the growing dark.

DEIRDRE BAKER is a highly regarded contributor to the *Horn Book* and the children's book reviewer for the *Toronto Star*. She has taught children's literature throughout Canada and the US and currently teaches in the English department at the University of Toronto. She is the co-author (with Ken Setterington) of *A Guide to Canadian Children's Books* as well as the upcoming *Follow That Broomstick: A Guide to the Best Fantasy Literature for Young Readers*, co-written with Michele Landsberg.

Deirdre spends her summers on British Columbia's Hornby Island – an island very much like Gran's.